MW00463790

ASSIGNED A MATE

GRACE GOODWIN

Copyright © 2016 by Grace Goodwin

Published by Stormy Night Publications and Design, LLC.
www.StormyNightPublications.com

Cover design by Korey Mae Johnson
www.koreymaejohnson.com

Images by The Killion Group and Bigstock/mikiel

All rights reserved.

1st Print Edition. March 2016

ISBN-13: 978-1530617074

ISBN-10: 1530617073

FOR AUDIENCES 18+ ONLY

This book is intended for adults only. Spanking and other sexual activities represented in this book are fantasies only, intended for adults.

CHAPTER ONE

My mind was fuzzy, as if I was just waking up or had too much alcohol in my system. But the fog was quickly chased away by sensation. I was naked and bent forward over some sort of hard bench. My breasts swayed below me with each powerful thrust of a man's cock deep into me. The stretching heat forced a moan from my throat and I closed my eyes to relish the way my tight pussy clenched and spasmed around his thick length. He stood behind me and I longed to see his face, to know who could give me such pleasure.

"She appears to like being fucked in such a manner. Most do not like being bent over and secured to a stand." A deep male voice spoke from somewhere behind me, but I was too distracted by the rough glide of the massive cock in and out of my body to look for him. He wasn't the man fucking me, and so he was nothing to me. Nothing. Only my master mattered.

Master? Where had that thought come from?

"Yes, her pussy is incredibly tight and dripping wet. Do you like being taken like this, *gara?*" The second voice was even deeper and came from behind me, directly behind me.

He had asked me a question, but all I could do was groan

at the way he spread me unbelievably wide. I'd never been speared by a cock this size. The hard heat bottomed out deep inside me with each hard slap of his hips against my ass. The sound of skin against skin, of my wetness easing his powerful passage, filled the room. He changed his angle, his hard head rubbing somewhere deep inside and I whimpered. His cock was like a weapon, a tool I was powerless to fight.

How had I gotten here? The last thing I remembered was being on Earth, in the processing center.

Now I was tied to some type of four-legged stand, my ankles bound to one side and my hands tied to small handles attached to the other. It was narrow enough that my breasts hung down, allowing something I couldn't see to tug on my nipples. The pain and pleasure combination was like an electrical current sent directly to my clit and I gasped at the sharp sensation. With every deep thrust, my clit ground against something hard beneath me, something that moved with me as his cock pounded into me. The vibrations under my clit caused an orgasm to build until I felt like a ticking time bomb. Sweat broke out on my skin and I clung to the stand as if it were the only thing keeping me from flying away. I wasn't entirely sure I was going to survive the explosion.

"She is squeezing my cock," the man growled and his motions became less methodical, as if he was losing his fight against his baser needs to rut into me.

"Good. Make her come hard so she will soften and accept your seed. You should be able to breed her without delay."

Breed?

I opened my mouth to ask what they were talking about, but that huge cock slammed into me and a warm hand came to rest on the back of my neck, holding me down, even though I could go nowhere. I felt it as a symbolic gesture, that I was under his control and could do nothing. I should have screamed or fought, but that hand acted like an off switch and I held myself completely still, eager for his next thrust.

This moment, this man… surely it was nothing more than a dream. I would *never* have sex with someone else watching. I would never allow myself to be tied and bound in such a manner. Never. This couldn't be real. I wouldn't allow this base treatment. I was a physician, a healer. Highly respected and not without means. I was a woman with some power. I would never submit to this…

As if to mock me, he slammed into me with extra force and a strong hand landed with a sting on my bare ass cheek. The burn spread like hot butter melting into my flesh, the heat traveling in a straight line to my clit. He spanked me again and I clenched my teeth to hold back a scream of pleasure.

What was happening to me? I *liked* being spanked?

Another loud smack, another sting of pain, and tears leaked from my eyes as I fought to maintain my composure. I was a professional. I never surrendered to panic or pressure. Or pleasure. I never lost control.

Drawing on years of training and discipline, I forced my mind to take note of my surroundings. I did not recognize anything, not the soft amber lighting, the thick carpets on the floor, the oddly sand-colored walls, or the scent of almonds and something strangely exotic that drifted to me from my own skin. The shining reflection of my normally pale flesh made it appear that I'd been rubbed down with scented oil. That smell—and the sticky musk of fucking—floated around me in the warm air.

Confusion filled my mind, but I couldn't focus on the room, or figure out how I got here because with every panted breath a hard cock filled me just to the brink of pain, close enough that the sharp hint of it only added to the sensations overloading my mind and body. I was consumed with pleasure. My entire awareness shrank until there was nothing but the press of my skin against the stand, the hand at my neck holding me in place like a contented cat, the pulling sway of what felt like small weights attached to my nipples, my pussy clenching at the cock that filled me, claimed me. Owned me.

Sex had never been this good with any of the men I'd been with. I couldn't see who was fucking me but there was no question he was a *man.*

The grip on the back of my neck vanished and I felt two large hands on my bare hips, the fingertips pressing into my round flesh. Since I couldn't see either man, this had to be a dream. And I didn't want it to end. I needed to come so badly I was ready to beg for release.

I'd never had a sex dream before. I'd never dreamt anything like this, where the dream seemed *so* real, felt *so* good. I didn't care, didn't want to think anything more about it because the vibrations against my clit sped up.

"Yes!" I cried, trying to push my hips back to take the incredible cock even deeper. "Don't stop, please, oh, God!"

He didn't. Like the delectable dream that it was, I came. The vibrations on my clit pushed me over the edge, but it was the cock filling me that kept the pleasure going and going until I couldn't take it anymore.

The man fucking me tensed, his fingers dug into my hips as he roared his own release. I felt his hot seed deep inside of me. As he continued to fuck me through his orgasm, the warm, sticky liquid seeped out of my pussy and down my thighs. I slumped over the stand, sated and replete. The last thing I heard before I slipped back into the darkness of dreams was, "She will do. Take her to the harem."

• • • • • • •

I fought my way back to awareness and wished I hadn't. A stern young woman sat opposite me in the small examination room. She appeared to be close to my age, and would have been pretty, if not for the thin-lipped, unsympathetic look on her face. She wore a crisp brown suit and high heels and held a computer processing tablet on her lap. With her long hair pulled back into a strict bun, she looked like a businesswoman, not a medical specialist. The room I was in looked like a hospital room, with medical equipment hooked up to my body to monitor my heart rate, brain activity, and enzyme levels. My body still hummed from the strength of my release and I was ashamed to notice that the examination chair I was strapped to was soaked beneath my bare ass and thighs, the wetness caused by arousal. The plain, short gray gown I wore was covered in the logo for the Interstellar Bride Program, and just like all standard medical garb was open in the back. As expected, I was naked beneath for processing.

The woman had the sour expression of someone who was used to dealing with prisoners who were truly guilty of their soulless crimes. Her dark brown uniform had the bright red insignia and three words in shimmering letters on her chest that made me break out in a cold sweat.

Interstellar Bride Program.

God help me. I was going off-world, leaving Earth behind as a mail-order bride. While the concept had been useful many centuries before, it was revitalized to meet current interplanetary needs. As one of these mail-order brides, I would be forced to fuck and make babies with some alien leader from a planet deemed worthy by the interstellar coalition that now protected Earth. An alien male who had earned the rank and the right to claim a bride from one of the protected member worlds. As Earth was the newest planet added to the coalition, it now offered the required thousand brides per year. There were very few volunteers, despite the generous compensation granted to a woman who was courageous—or desperate—enough to volunteer to be a bride. No, most of the thousand brides sent off-world were women convicted of a crime, or like me, forced to run. To hide.

"*...you should be able to breed her without delay.*" That rough, hard-edged voice drifted through my mind. That had been just a dream, right? But why would I dream *that*?

5

"Miss Day, I am Warden Egara. Are you aware of your placement options? As a convicted murderer, you forfeit all rights but the right of naming. You may name a world, if you wish, and we will choose your mate from that world based on your assessment results. Or you may waive the right of naming and accept the results of the psychological assessment process. If you choose this option, you will be sent to the world, and the mate, that best matches your psychological profile. If you wish to meet your true mate, I highly recommend you choose the second option and follow the recommendations of the matching processors. We have been matching brides and their mates for hundreds of years. Which is it to be?"

The woman's voice barely registered and I pulled against the cuffs that locked my wrists at my sides. While I'd heard mention of other planets, I didn't know anyone from another world, especially not a mate. On Earth a woman could choose her own boyfriends, lovers, husbands. But an alien mate? I had no idea where to start. And even if I chose a world, my actual match would be decided solely through the Interstellar Bride Program's psychological analysis. Should I pick a world? I was only going to be gone for a few months, not the rest of my life. What difference did it make? I wasn't even really Evelyn Day.

It was my new identity. My real name was Eva Daily and I wasn't really a murderer, either. I was innocent, but that didn't matter. Not anymore. It didn't matter that this was all a farce, a way to keep me alive until a trial date could be set and I could testify against a member of one of the most powerful organized crime syndicates on Earth.

I'd been a well-respected doctor until I witnessed a murder behind a curtain in the hospital's emergency department. Turned out, I was the only one who could identify the assassin. The killer's family had immense wealth and powerful connections in both the world's government and organized crime. Witness protection was the only chance of keeping me alive until I could identify the man in court. Going off-planet was the only way to ensure the family's extensive reach wouldn't harm me.

Regardless of the fact that my conviction was just a cover, as far as Earth's justice system was concerned, I was a murderer. I was to be treated as such. This medical gown was plain gray prison garb, my wrist and ankles were both bound to a hard, unforgiving chair. I was out of options. I'd already gone through this a thousand times in my head. Survive. That's what I had to do and there was no way to do that if I didn't get away from Earth as quickly as possible.

"Miss Day?" the warden repeated. Her voice was emotionless, as if she'd processed too many criminals to be anything but jaded and hardened to the worst offenders.

"I will ask once more, Miss Day. Three is the required number of times I must attempt to elicit a response. After that, you will automatically be matched based on the results of your testing and submitted for processing."

I tried to calm my racing heart, for I was not only bound in place, I couldn't escape the room, the building and most especially, the life I now had to face. This drab room was nothing compared to what I'd already endured… and nothing to what was still to come.

But I couldn't let this cold-hearted woman choose for me. Surely she'd send me to a harsh planet like Prillon, where the men were notorious for being hard and unforgiving, both in bed and out of it.

"Do you wish to claim the right of naming your world, Miss Day? Or do you submit to the processing center's placement protocols?" Her prompt brought me out of my thoughts. Before she'd entered the room, I'd been subjected to their so-called processing. I'd been fully alert and awake when it started, watching images of various landscapes, men in all kinds of dress and appearance, even couples participating in various sexual acts, such as a woman on her knees and sucking a man's cock.

Unfortunately, that had been one of the tamer images. Some images included two men taking a woman, some an entire room full of people watching as one woman was fucked. Bondage, floggers, sexual aids. The scenes had gone from deserts to pictures of the urban expanses of huge alien cities the size of New York City or London, from dildos and chastity belts to piercings and anal probes.

The images had moved faster and faster and I thought I'd remained awake, but I must have fallen asleep and had that weird, yet vivid, dream. When I awoke, the video screens were gone, but I was still bound to the examination chair.

I glanced up at her neutral expression, licked my lips, and replied, "I will accept the processing protocol selection."

The woman gave a curt nod as she pressed a button on the tablet before her. "Very good. Let's begin the placement selection protocol. For the record, state your name."

I closed my eyes for a moment, then opened them, for I could still feel the lingering effects of that orgasm. It had been intense and it had been a *dream*. This was cold, hard reality. I doubted there would be real escape, or any real pleasure in my future. "E-Evelyn Day."

I'd been about to say my real name, but remembered myself. *How could I forget?*

"The crime for which you've been found guilty?"

It was hard to say the word. I still couldn't believe I had agreed to such extreme measures, such lies. "Murder."

"Are you currently, or have you ever been married?"

"No." That was one of the reasons I was in this mess. I worked too much. I had no man in my life, no one to come home to. So I stayed at work, took extra shifts, and witnessed a murder.

"Have you produced biological offspring?"

"No." I wanted to, someday, but with an alien? That hadn't been in my childhood dreams. Why couldn't I have met a sexy, single man who liked a woman with both a brain and generous curves?

"Excellent." Warden Egara checked off a list of boxes on her display tablet. "For the record, Miss Day, as an eligible, fertile female in your prime, you had two options available to you to serve out your sentence for the crime of murder, life without parole in a Carswell Penitentiary located in Fort Worth, Texas."

I shivered at the mention of the notorious prison that housed the most dangerous and cruelest of criminals. The entire plan to keep me safe until trial was to send me off-planet. Carswell, fortunately, wasn't something I had to consider.

Warden Egara continued, "Or, as you chose earlier, the alternative of the Interstellar Bride Program. You were brought here to complete your assessment and matching. I am pleased to tell you that the system has made a successful match and you will be sent to a member planet. As a bride, you might never return to Earth, as all travel will be determined and controlled by your new planet's laws and customs. You will surrender your citizenship of Earth and become an official citizen of your new world."

Where would they send me? What kind of perverted insanity had my neuroscans shown this woman? Based on the vivid dream, it could have been anything. Would I go to a chieftain on Vytros or a rich merchant captain on Ania? One of the rough, patriarchal, outlier worlds?

I cleared my throat, for the words seemed stuck. "Can you… can you explain the choosing process? How do I know the tests made a good match?"

She looked at me as if I'd lived under a rock my entire life. "Really, Miss Day. You know how it works."

When I remained silent, she sighed. "Very well. All prisoners are put through a series of tests. Your mind has been stimulated and monitored for both conscious and subconscious reactions so that we can make sure to match you appropriately with another planet's customs and sexual practices. As you will be living there indefinitely, it is important that we send brides that are *worthy* of the leaders who request them.

"Each planet has a list of qualified males awaiting a

bride," she continued. "Your testing discovers the best world for you, then matches you to the most compatible candidate. Once your processing begins, he is immediately notified. Once done, you will be transported and you will awaken on your new planet. Your mate will be waiting to claim you."

My wrists were still bound; I was able to clench my fists. "What if... what if the match isn't good?"

She pursed her lips. "There is no coming back. Per Protocol 6.2.7a, we can't force you to remain with someone incompatible. You will have thirty days to decide if the primary candidate is acceptable. If, after thirty days, you are not satisfied with your mate, you will be assigned another mate on that world and transferred. You will have thirty days to accept or reject each candidate until you settle down with a mate."

"Do they... I mean, does he have the opportunity to reject me?" I'd been rejected by men. Many times. What would make a man on some far-off planet be any different?

"The matching program's success rate is well over ninety-eight percent. You have completed the testing and we have confirmed your personal placement. I am confident you will be settled sufficiently. These mates, depending on the planet, need women to sustain their race, their culture, and their way of life. Females are valuable, Miss Day. This is why the interplanetary treaty was put in place. If, however, your mate finds you... unsatisfactory, you will be matched to another male on that world. Remember, you were matched to the world first, the mate second."

"Will my mate know that I've been convicted of a crime?"

"Of course. The treaty demands full disclosure."

"And they're desperate enough to accept convicts?" I had never been found worthy enough to be a girlfriend, let alone a wife. Why would someone want me now that I was a convicted murderer? "Aren't they afraid that I might murder them in their sleep?" I wouldn't do that, but surely *they* didn't know that. And would I be punished on their world for a crime I had supposedly committed here, on Earth?

The woman pursed her lips. "I guarantee, Miss Day, that when you meet any of the mates on any of the planets, you will understand. Rest assured that being murdered by a woman such as yourself will not be one of their concerns."

I glanced down at myself in the drab, plain prison garb. I wasn't a waif. I was... curvy. Even the stress of the past couple weeks, the upcoming trial and all that entailed, hadn't changed my weight. I hadn't seen a real mirror or any makeup in that time, so I could only imagine what I looked like. If I ended up with my mate looking like this, surely he'd refuse me even before he said hello.

The woman glanced at her tablet. "Are you done with your questions? I have another woman to process today."

There really wasn't much choice. I nodded. "I'm... I'm ready—" I swallowed. It was harder than I thought it would be to say the words that would change my life. "I'm ready to go off-planet and I will accept placement based on the testing."

The woman nodded decisively. "Very well." She pushed a button and my chair angled back as if I were at the dental technician. "For the record, Miss Day, you have chosen to serve out your sentence under the direction of the Interstellar Bride Program. You have been assigned to a mate per testing protocols and will be transported off-planet, never to return to Earth. Is this correct?"

Holy mother of God, what had I done? I would come back to testify, but I was *really* going. "Yes."

"Excellent." She glanced down at her tablet. "The computer has assigned you to Trion."

Trion? I scrambled through my memories looking for something, anything about that world. Nothing. I had nothing. *Oh, God.*

But maybe that world had been the one in my dream. The rugs. The almond oil. The huge cock...

"That world requires detailed physical preparation for their females. Therefore, your body must be properly prepared before we initiate transport."

My body will be… what?

Warden Egara pushed the side of my chair and to my shock, the chair slid toward the wall where a large opening appeared. The examination chair slid, as if on a track, right into the newly revealed space on the other side of the wall. The tiny room was small, and glowing with a series of bright blue lights. The chair lurched to a stop and a robotic arm with a large needle slid silently up to my neck. I winced as it pierced my skin, then all I felt was a slight tingling at the injection site. A sense of lethargy and contentment made my body go limp as I was lowered into a bath of warm blue liquid. I was so warm, so numb…

"Just try to relax, Miss Day." Her finger touched the display in her hand and her voice drifted to me as if from far, far away. "Your processing will begin in three… two… one…"

CHAPTER TWO

"The transfer must be wearing on the body, therefore she sleeps."

I heard the voice, but didn't stir. I was quite comfortable and I didn't want to wake up.

"Yes, however, she has been like that for four hours." This voice was deeper, more commanding, clearly frustrated by my state. "Goran, perhaps my mate was damaged in transport."

Damaged?

"There does not appear to be any damage." A different voice. "She is small and perhaps needs additional time to recover."

Small? I'd *never* been considered small. Short, maybe, but small? That was almost funny. I couldn't will my body to move, to see who considered me to be anything but my usual curvy, very solid self. It was as if I'd woken up from a long nap and I was content to stay that way. I felt warm and safe and secure, not on the brink of... oh!

My eyes fluttered open and I did not see the stark gray walls of the interior of the processing facility where I'd spent the past few days. Instead, I seemed to be in some sort of rustic structure, the ceiling and walls made out of sturdy canvas. I couldn't see much of the space, for there were three men looming over me. My eyes widened at their size. They were formidably large and... *large*. I'd never seen a man so big, let alone three of them. Was their size normal?

Everything about them was dark. Black hair and eyes, black clothing over tanned skin. They reminded me of men from the Mediterranean region of Europe. But I had not been sent by the processing center to Europe, or even the mid-East, but off-planet. Trion? Where was that? How far was I from home? Warden Egara hadn't said how far away this planet was before she'd swiped her finger across her display and had me transported. It had happened so fast, like falling asleep for a surgery and waking up afterward completely unaware of everything that had happened in between.

I was lying on my side, no longer in that uncomfortable chair in the processing room, but on a narrow bed. My wrists and ankles were no longer restrained and I reached up and threaded the fingertips of my right hand through the hair just behind my ear.

Yes. There it was. I released a pent-up breath. The small lump caused by the justice department's implant, the device that they'd promised would bring me home someday. Until then, I had to survive as Evelyn Day, convicted murderer.

I blinked, confused, as I tried to get my bearings. I'd known about alternate planets my entire life, but images of them on the media were never provided. Transport off-planet was only allowed for military personnel or for women in the bride program. Because of this, I'd always imagined that aliens would be very different than humans, but I was most definitely wrong. These men, if they were examples of their planet's race, were very handsome specimens and very human-like. Handsome perhaps wasn't the correct word. Intense, virile, manly. Gorgeous.

Regardless, their power and harsh energy, their sheer size, and the very distinct possibility that they might hurt me had me scrambling backwards.

The wall was pliant against my back and I had to put my hand down to balance myself. I was on my hands and knees and the men's gazes dropped from my face to my body. While the air was warm—wherever I was—I felt it against my bare skin. Looking down, I was definitely not in prison garb. I was naked.

"Where are my clothes?" I squeaked, trying to cover myself and looking around. The space was Spartan, containing only the bed where I sat and a table in the center of the space. The room wasn't overly large, or perhaps it was the sheer size of the three men before me taking up most of the space. Large black trunks lined a wall and metal gadgets, looking like medical machinery from the hospital and appliances from my kitchen, sat upon them.

"You have been transported and processed as custom demands," one of the men said.

"But, I'm naked." My hands froze and I looked down when I felt my nipples. They had gold rings through them. If that weren't enough, a gold chain ran from one ring to the other and hung down to just above my navel.

I... um, I had nipple piercings. I couldn't turn my gaze from the strange sight. The hoops were smaller than a ring meant for a finger, the chain attached was thin like a cord and decorated with small gold discs.

"I see by your reaction that being adorned is not a custom on Earth." I didn't look up to see who spoke.

Adorned? Surprisingly, the nipple piercings didn't hurt, even though they were brand new. Surely they would be sore. When I was ten I'd had my ears pierced and it had taken well over a month for the holes to heal. I felt no pain now, only a slight pulling on them because of the weight of the chain. It was slight, but constant... and arousing. My nipples tightened and I gasped, crossing my arms over my chest.

"Welcome to Trion. I am Tark, your new master, and you are in the med unit at Outpost Nine. I brought you here to see the doctor after your transfer, for you did not wake."

The one on the right spoke, his voice deep and somehow familiar. His dark eyes met mine and held. I couldn't look away, nor did I want to, for I felt... something. No man on Earth ever looked at me in such an intense way. It was as if he were claiming me solely with his eyes.

Why would his voice sound familiar? Odd, but I shook that thought away as impossible. He glanced at one of the other men, then looked at me again, clearly and intently. "This is Goran, my second-in-command." The other man nodded to me. He appeared younger than Tark and an inch or two shorter, but no less powerful of build. "And this is Bron, the doctor stationed here at Outpost Nine."

The third man offered a slight head tilt as well and remained silent. He didn't keep his eyes on mine as Tark did, but let them rove over my body. I shifted my hands to cover myself better, but knew he could see *everything*.

All three wore black pants, but while the other two men wore black shirts, Tark's was gray. The cut was similar to what Earth men wore, yet I'd never seen such broad shoulders or well-defined bodies. These were strong men and their clothing only accentuated that.

Tark was the only man who spoke to me. "Evelyn Day, you have been matched to me by the interplanetary treaty. While I have been assured of your wellness, the transfer could have harmed you. You were asleep for more time than anticipated. Bron will examine you for any damage. Up."

He held out his large hand for me to take. I eyed it, then him, carefully. Warily.

"Examine me?" I asked, my eyes widening further. I could hear the rush of blood in my ears and I began to pant. "There's... there's no need. As you said, I'm just... small."

He took a step closer, kept his hand out. "I disagree. I take care of what's mine."

Patiently, he waited, then sighed.

"I understand an Earth prison was your alternative. I am pleased with your choice, for out of all the possible mates in the Interplanetary Treaty, your subconscious needs were best matched to our way of life. It seems we are to give each other exactly what we both need."

He paused and I let those words sink in. Would he give me what I needed? How could he, when what I needed was to go home, testify, and get my old life back?

He reached forward and ran his knuckles down my cheek. "Your past is unimportant, *gara*. You are mine now, and you must obey me in all things." His voice dropped lower and his tone said that he would not be denied.

I frowned, not pleased with his words, but the tender touch had me off-kilter.

I took his hand because I had no choice. It was so big, my palm engulfed by his. The touch was warm, the clasp gentle, but I doubted he'd let me tug away. I couldn't get past the men if I wished to run, and if I did evade them, I still didn't even know where I was. The only way to return to Earth was through the transporter, and they wouldn't take me to a transport outpost, nor did I know how to operate one. I was well and truly stuck with *him*. At least until I was called back to testify. The prosecutor said that it could take months, however. *Months* with this man on a strange planet? I gulped.

He helped me to my feet and I swayed, the chain dangling from my breasts shifting as well. I stood on what felt like a sheet of thin gray flooring. It did not cover the entire space, for sand ringed it all the way to the walls. Sand? Were we in the desert? Was that why it was warm, why their skin was so nicely tanned? The sight of my bare feet next to three sets of boots looked odd.

The walls were opaque. Lights on stands around the room cast a soft glow.

I put my free hand up to stop the motion. He steadied me as I tilted my head back, way back, to meet his gaze. "What... what are you going to do with me?"

His dark eyes searched my face, then moved lower down my body. I flushed, knowing he—and the others—could see everything.

"You are the first we have seen from Earth and I must have a closer look." The doctor's gaze roved over my body just as Tark's had, but he made me feel… exposed and dirty. I knew that look. Lecherous men, it seemed, were not limited to Earth.

I moved to stand slightly behind Tark, using him as a shield. His scent lifted from his shirt and it was intoxicating. Clean, sharp and with a hint of something mysterious. Whatever it was, I liked it. Was it because we'd been matched?

"I do not need to be examined and you most certainly won't have a closer look. I am well, or they would not have sent me. I am also not a science experiment. I am a mate." I tipped my chin up and firmed my voice, but I was at the mercy of these men. I had no idea if the term mate held any sort of status on Trion, but surely no man would allow another to *examine* his mate for enjoyment alone.

I didn't look up, but I could see that Tark glanced from me to the two men before me.

"You allow her to speak to me in such a way?" Bron asked Tark, his expression venomous toward me.

Tark's other hand clenched into a fist. "Shall I allow you to examine *my* mate with a cock stand in your pants?"

The man shifted himself and had the decency to look embarrassed.

Tark lifted his hand in a dismissive wave and I felt more than heard a growl deep in his chest. "Goran, take him out of here. I will check my mate on my own."

Goran nodded and grabbed the doctor's arm, tugging him away. With one last narrowed glance over his shoulder, Bron was led out of the tent through a flap on the far wall. I briefly saw the shapes of other tents, but the view was quickly blocked once again.

Now alone with me, Tark turned to look down on me, a towering warrior hungry for his bride. I couldn't believe this man was my mate. While I'd dreamed of finding someone special, it was quite different to know in advance that he was *the one.* There was no dating, no courtship to discover common interests and compatibility. It was actually very unnerving. Add to that, I was on a new planet halfway across the galaxy!

I could hear things through the thin walls: voices, odd mechanical noises, unusual sounds that had to come from animals. Perhaps horses? What kind of animals did they have on Trion?

"What Bron said is true. You are not to speak to him in such a way."

My eyes widened. "He wasn't acting as a doctor should," I countered.

He took a moment, as if considering. "You are new here and therefore I will take that into account regarding your punishment."

"Punish—"

He raised a hand and cut me off. "Impertinence is not allowed."

I frowned. "*He* was the one who was impertinent."

Tark rolled his shoulders back and appeared to have grown an inch. "Who is being impertinent now?"

He took two steps with his long legs to a simple, short bench. It appeared to be made of wood, but I had no idea if that was true. Did they even have trees on Trion?

When he sat down, he held out his hand. "Come."

I looked at his fingers, long and blunt, but did not move. "Why?"

"I will give you your first lesson about Trion."

That seemed reasonable considering I had only been on the planet for about five minutes. I closed the distance between us. Before I knew what had happened, he grabbed me about the waist and placed me over his lap. I was not a small woman and he did the maneuvering as if I were a petite waif.

My hips were over his hard thighs, my upper body bent toward the gray flooring, my breasts hanging down. The chain that dangled between them brushed against the floor.

My toes touched the floor and I tried to push up.

"What are you doing?" I cried, the blood rushing to my head. "Let me up!"

Tark placed a warm hand at the small of my back to hold me on his lap and as I tried to kick, he hooked my ankles with one of his legs.

"Settle, *gara*. I expected you to have a punishment lesson soon enough, but not this quickly."

"Punishment?" I shouted. "I thought you said you were going to teach me about Trion!"

"I am. Starting with this."

I heard the crack of his hand against my bottom before I felt it. The sharp sting of it sizzled across my bare flesh.

"Tark! Cut it out, you overbearing... jerk!"

He spanked me again. And again. Each time his large palm struck, it was in a new spot. Soon enough my skin felt as if it were on fire, stinging and hot.

I was breathing hard, my hair falling down over my face and I swiped to get it out of the way. On one decidedly hard smack of his hand, I reached back and tried to cover my bottom. Instead of deterring him, he only circled my wrists in his free hand and continued.

"Are you ready to listen... with your mouth closed?" he asked, stroking over my heated skin. Surely it was bright red and swollen.

Afraid to say a word, I just nodded my head, then slumped down across his lap.

"Ah, *gara*. Your submission is a pleasure to see." Before I could even begin to think about that statement, he continued. "We speak with deference here on Trion. I believe it is also referred to as manners."

I tugged a strand of hair out of my mouth as I realized Tark considered me mannerless. What did he think, that Earth was full of heathens?

"It is not for you to argue with the doctor. It is my job to do so in your stead. He was impertinent, as you said, but it was my job as your mate to defend your honor. To defend your position as a woman in this society. To protect you. When you spoke out of turn, you took that from me, thus dishonoring me as well."

It was a tad antiquated, but I could understand the logic. I stroked my fingers over the smooth flooring. Having a conversation with my face near the floor was odd, but so was being spanked. Well, so was being on Trion for that matter. "You mean that I am to defer to you?"

"Are you familiar with the ways and customs of Trion?"

I shook my head.

"Are you familiar with me?"

I shook my head again.

"Doctor Bron or the examination he was going to give?"

"No," I replied.

"If I were to appear on Earth, wouldn't you wish to speak for me, to help guide me as I learned my way?"

I clenched my teeth again and hated that his reasoning was not unfounded.

"Yes."

He released his hold on my wrists and helped me to stand before him, close enough to be situated between his spread knees. My bottom was hot and stung from the spanking. His size was great enough that his eyes were not in line with my breasts. That did not mean that I did not feel any less exposed and vulnerable, even more so now that he pointed out the error of my ways.

"I need to check your implant."

His words stirred me from my thoughts. I was surprised that he could switch to another topic so readily. He'd meted out my punishment and it was time to move on?

"I assume your neuroprocessor is working properly, since you seem to understand everything said to you."

I frowned. "What?" What was he talking about? What neuroprocessor?

"Do not be afraid, small one." I was average height and at least two dress sizes bigger than the medical charts on Earth said I should be. I was not *small*, but standing in front of my new mate, I felt almost tiny, and very, very female.

Tark lifted his hands to my head and ran his fingers up the sides of my face to the top of each temple, just above my eyes. He must have found what he was looking for because when he applied a very small amount of pressure, I felt two foreign bumps pressing into the bone of my skull. It wasn't painful, but definitely odd.

"What is that?" The moment Tark removed his hands, I lifted my own shaking fingers to the same spots and felt the small bumps beneath my skin.

"They are advanced neuroprocessing units, or NPUs. All advanced member races of the Interstellar Bride Program have them implanted at birth. The NPU increases your brain's ability to process and learn language and mathematics, and improves memory. We are speaking now in my planet's common tongue, which was downloaded to your NPU before you arrived."

Holy shit. I was a cyborg or something now?

"I have alien technology implanted in my head? Are there little wires running to my brain cells? How did the NPU system integrate and communicate with the organic tissue?" My medically trained mind had a hundred questions and no answers.

Tark's eyes widened and his lip quirked. "Aren't you the curious one?"

Instead of answering my questions, he glanced at the table in the middle of the room. "Lie down again, Evelyn Day." His voice was still deep, but lacked the biting edge he'd had when spanking me.

I couldn't avoid my mate or what he planned to do to me. I could try, but decided against it because my bottom was very sore and still suffering the consequences of my previous actions. While the doctor had pricked my ire, Tark made me feel something else entirely. I wasn't happy that he'd spanked me—absolutely not—but he did make a clear argument and I *had* been in the wrong. I liked that he'd given the punishment, then moved on. I, too, felt I should move on from it as well. Learn from it, of course, for I didn't wish to go through that again. I reached back and gently rubbed my hot skin.

Odd. There was something about him, his power, his protectiveness—he had protected me from the doctor—and his dominance that was very appealing. Looking at how well his large body was defined in his dark clothes, I wanted to please him. Besides that, I itched to run my hands over his arms to feel his biceps, over his broad shoulders, down his chest. Surely his abdominals would be hard and well defined. And lower…

I went over to the table and Tark followed. With his hands at my hips, he lifted me up onto the metal surface and I hissed at the cool contact with my overheated bottom.

"Lie back," Tark told me.

Licking my lips, I settled back onto the table as I watched his eyes rove over my body. Unlike the doctor, Tark looked at me with arousal, definitely, but also something like reverence. I keenly felt the heated slide of his gaze, as if his fingers were actually tracing the curves of my flesh.

"As I said, you must be examined to ensure you are well. I have plans for you, *gara*."

I could do nothing but lick my dry lips at the raspy sound of his voice.

"I will touch you now."

I gasped when his hand cupped my breast, for the touch was gentle, yet I felt rough calluses on his palm.

He watched as my nipple tightened, then rubbed his thumb back and forth over the taut peak, shifting the gold ring.

"Why… why the rings?" I asked, my voice soft. I shivered at the idea of a stranger—who was also my mate—touching me.

"We adorn our women and find the rings both beautiful and arousing." He watched my breast as he replied. "All of our mates have rings placed in their nipples. It is a sign of claiming and respect."

"They don't hurt," I said.

He smiled then. "I hope not. My touch should bring you pleasure, *gara*, nothing else."

No, they didn't hurt at all. Instead, the soft tug and pull of the metal felt incredible. My nipples had always been sensitive, but now, I arched my back to press into his palm more fully.

"You were processed according to our social customs. It normally takes several weeks for the rings to heal and I had no intention of waiting that long before I touched you... here." He flicked the ring and I gasped. "A perk of the transfer... for both of us."

"And the chain?"

Tark lifted the chain and I noticed a small crest had been stamped into several tiny golden disks that were woven into the shining strand. "This symbol is my birthing mark, and the mark of my line. It signifies that you are mine. Until I claim you and mark you permanently, it is also your protection."

"Protection?" I didn't understand how rings in my nipples were going to protect me from anything, but the way he continued to play, I didn't really care.

"No one will dare touch what belongs to the high councilor." He sounded like a possessive caveman. "Enough questions. Place your hands above your head and allow me to examine my mate."

I froze, my hands locked in front of me. "Tark, I don't—"

"This..." He moved his hand a little lower and gently tugged on the chain, sending a hot sizzle of pleasure from both of my nipples directly to my clit, "...is also a tool I will use to make sure you learn obedience, *gara*. Just one of the many ways your body will learn to submit to mine—and keep you from arguing."

He let go of the chain and it fell onto my skin once again, the once cool metal now heated by his touch. Tark gently wrapped each of my wrists in his big, strong hands and

24

slowly maneuvered me until my hands were above my head on the exam table, as he'd requested.

"Or, I can flip you over onto your belly and spank you once again. It is your choice."

I almost rolled my eyes and realized he would definitely consider that impertinence.

"That is not much of a choice," I grumbled.

He offered a small smile. "You are learning quickly, *gara*. Know this, I will never harm you. But I will also never allow you to hurt yourself. Bron—" he spit out the man's name, "—is new to my service, and after how he behaved, I will summon a new medical officer immediately upon our return to the palace. I wouldn't let him treat my *frim*, let alone my mate."

So he hadn't been taking the doctor's side earlier. Had I just remained quiet earlier, Tark would have dismissed the man and I would have been in this exact spot—without the sore bottom.

Tark's dark gaze drifted up from my thrusting breasts to my face. "I am going to touch you now, and you must tell me if you have any pain or discomfort from your transfer."

His hands stroked down my bare arms to my breasts, across the curves of my ribcage to my hips. Goosebumps broke out across my skin. He was learning my body like I was a fascinating specimen, something he had never seen before, and not necessarily in a sexual way. But his gentle touch calmed my fear, and without fear to hide behind, I could not stop myself from focusing on other things.

The heat of his hands. The racing of my heart. His touch was like fire on my flesh and he was *very* thorough. Despite the mental argument against allowing a stranger to touch me so intimately, and despite all the stress of the last few weeks, my body knew what to do and what it wanted. It responded with a desire so swift it shocked me. His hand moved up my legs and slipped between my thighs.

I gasped at the light contact, my body arched off the table as if he'd applied an electrical shock. I squeezed my knees together, pinning his hand in place. He released his hold on my wrists and traced the soft curve of my abdomen until he found the chain and gave a soft tug. I cried out and closed my eyes. The sight of him over me, so dominant, so intense, made me consider things I would never, ever think to do. Like allow a complete stranger to play with my pussy. No, not allow, want. I wanted my mate to touch me.

What the hell was wrong with me? Had the transfer made me lose my mind? Had it made me horny? Was there some kind of sexual neuroprocessor stimulant that upped my libido? But then again, it could just be the testosterone oozing from his pores.

"Open your legs, *gara*. Now. Do not be afraid."

"I'm not… I don't…" I wasn't afraid that he'd harm me. Quite the opposite. I was afraid of myself, afraid that I'd give him anything he wanted. I didn't know him at all, but his gentle hands and firm commands threatened to break down all of my barriers, break all of my rules about men. And I'd just met him.

I felt him move closer, and his mouth closed over my nipple; the swirl of his tongue pulling on the small ring made me moan with pleasure. "Open for me, mate. Let me see what is mine."

His touch. His kiss. His heat.

My mate. Mine. He belonged to me as much as I belonged to him. At least for now.

I let my knees fall wide and opened my eyes as he moved away from my breast and closer to my core.

Coming up on my elbows, I looked down my body and my eyes widened once again. "I have no hair." I'd thought it had felt different… down there, but I'd been too distracted by the nipple rings and chain and the spanking to notice my pussy had been made bare.

"It is sensitive for you, yes?" He asked the question, then bent low to blow a soft breath of air over my pussy lips. He may not have touched a woman from Earth before, but he certainly knew what he was doing. He blew on me again and

I shuddered. He was staring now, his face so close that he could surely pick up my own scent and I wondered...

"Am I... shaped like the women on your planet?"

"Mmm."

I thought he would ignore my question, but apparently, he had decided to investigate. Tark lifted something from the side of the table, and moments later a cold, hard object was slowly inserted into my core. I pushed with legs and arms in a scramble to get away.

"Stop. What are you doing to me?"

"Don't move."

I shook my head, startled and surprised at the object. He grabbed my wrists once again and easily secured them into cuffs at the top of the table. Angling my head back, I looked up at my constraints. Tugging at them, it was no use. There was no give. It was like in the dream at the processing center, bound and a man touching me. I could feel my pussy getting wet at the memory. I struggled against them and that only made me wetter, my arousal slipping out around the dildo that filled me. I was bound with a man looming over me, the sheer size of him capable of doing me harm, but all he wanted to do was give me pleasure—strange, unknown, and scary pleasure. My bottom was sore from his earlier spanking and I could do nothing but submit.

Tark's large palm settled across my abdomen as a strange whirring sensation started in my core, followed by a heat that spread from my pussy to my ass, deep inside my womb, up through my outer pussy lips and higher, to my clit, striking there like a small electric shock. This was like no vibrator I'd ever seen—or felt—before.

"Ah!" My hips bucked at the overwhelming sensation and Tark's dark gaze seemed to be hypnotized, watching my reactions.

The strange device in my pussy beeped three times, then zapped my clit again. There was no other word I could think of to describe it. It didn't hurt, far from it actually. It felt incredible, and that was the problem. "Give in, mate.

27

Submit to the exam just as you are learning to submit to me."

CHAPTER THREE

"This isn't an exam. This is—" A strong electrical surge pulsed through the walls of my pussy to my ass, and I fought to maintain control of my body, but another zap to my clit sent me over the edge. The walls of my pussy and lower abdomen pulsed and spasmed so strongly I felt like I was coming apart. "Oh, God."

My body bucked on the table, beyond my control. I struggled against the bonds on my wrists. Shivering and spent, I turned my face away from my new mate. I tried to catch my breath as I fought back tears. The device inside me quieted to a small, nearly imperceptible hum. But after the overwhelming shock of the forced orgasm, that small vibration was easy to ignore.

Tark's pressure on my abdomen and thighs lifted and he reached down between my legs to remove the alien object from my pussy. I wanted to run and hide, but I was bound. How could I have responded like that to a stupid little medical tool? What had he done to me?

He looked at a display screen attached to the blunt silver tool and nodded his head. "Excellent, Evelyn Day. The medical probe indicates you are fertile, free of disease, and both your reproductive and nervous systems are functioning at optimal levels."

"Let me go." I tried to close my legs, but he held them open at the knees.

Looking up at me with his dark eyes, he said, "You are mine now and I won't let you go. Not when your body is so very eager to know me."

"Eager?" I questioned. "You forced that pleasure upon me. Look at me! I'm bound to the table and my bottom, my bottom is sore." A tear slid down my cheek.

Wiping it away from his finger, he responded, "The tests had to be done. There is nothing wrong with enjoying a small taste of pleasure while submitting to them. Submitting to me."

A strong, blunt finger traced my folds and I was embarrassed to feel how easily it glided through my wetness. "See? It makes you wet. Being bound and open for me is what you like."

"How would you know?" I countered.

"Because you are my mate. Do not question or fight what is a perfect match." He found my clit and my hips tilted toward him, his to command and eager for his curious touch. Clearly, my body and mind were not in synch.

"You are, indeed, much like our females. You should enjoy my finger here… and here."

I shook my head. "I-I shouldn't," I countered.

He used three fingers now, his thumb on my clit as he slid two more deep inside.

"You are allowed to come from my touch, even if we do not know each other. Our bodies, our minds, our very souls are connected. Give up, *gara*."

My arms began to shake and I relaxed on the table. He finger fucked me and found that sensitive spot inside. While the probe had brought about intense pleasure, his fingers elicited something else entirely. They were much more adept and a part of him. Still aroused from my *examination*, I moaned and rolled my hips beneath his hand, eager for more, unable to deny my body's desperate need to come all over his hand.

"Yes, you are very similar. Ah, my mate, I can tell by your reaction that I have found the secret place inside you that will drive your pleasure. See? I've kept your hands in the restraints because I know you like it. It heightens your pleasure."

He'd found it all right, and every other secret place that made me hot. If he kept at it much longer, he'd make me come again. I was panting now, and wet, and mortified that I'd reacted so strongly to him. A complete stranger. This couldn't be happening to me. There had to be some rational explanation. "Do they drug the women when they transfer them?"

"No." His gaze changed instantly, from generous and indulgent to cold and insulted. "We do not drug our women for pleasure. As you can feel, it is not necessary. Is that what the cowards on Earth do to their mates?"

"Some of them." I had insulted him, and I hadn't meant to. But seriously, what in the name of all that was holy was happening to me? "I'm sorry, I just…"

"No man of worth needs drugs to seduce his mate." He slowly and deliberately removed his hand from my pussy and I felt abandoned. Needy. Weak. Reaching up, he released one wrist, then the other from the bonds. As tears gathered once again in my eyes, I knew that, without a doubt, I was losing my freaking mind. Maybe the last few days had finally caught up to me. The murder I'd witnessed. The plan to send me off-planet to stay hidden and safe. The new identity and processing. The terror of being sent to a new world, to a man I'd never met.

"I'm sorry, Tark. I didn't mean to offend."

"You are tired and on a new world." I watched now as he put his glistening fingers in his mouth and grinned.

Oh, my God, he was tasting me. It was a very erotic sight and I clenched my thighs together to ease the ache.

"Sweet. Like the *rova* fruit."

I couldn't respond, for what did I say to a man who'd

just licked my pussy juices from his fingers?

"While you were asleep, Bron's standard scans picked up no other medical problems. As you responded to this last exam with only pleasure—no pain—I will assume the transfer was just too much for your fragile female body to endure without rest."

I could only nod. I should feel shame or fear or embarrassment at having Tark touch me so intimately. I was still naked, exposed, and vulnerable and definitely under his control. I felt all of those things, but my mind and my body were at war because his touch made my body feel safe, desirable, and very, very aroused.

I didn't know Goran had returned until he spoke. "The doctor is on the last convoy to Outpost Seventeen."

Tark didn't turn his head from me. "Good. Is everything ready?"

"Yes, sir."

Tark set aside the silver probe, stood to his full height, reached down and scooped me up, placing me on my feet before him. I could now see what the instrument looked like. It was definitely an otherworldly dildo. If they sold them on Earth, Tark would make a fortune.

Goran handed Tark a blanket and he wrapped it about me like a cape.

"From this moment on, your body belongs to me. No other man shall see what is mine without permission. Do you understand?"

Without permission? Did that mean he would allow it? I was confused, but before I could question, he lifted me into his arms and carried me out of the tent, following Goran. The air was warm and dry, but it was dark outside, the only light provided by small solar stakes that glowed in precise intervals along the ground. I could just see the outline of numerous tents. Tark and Goran both moved like ghosts, their footsteps quiet. Not many people were about; perhaps it was very late at night. An animal noise, something like a braying donkey, broke through the stillness. The men's footsteps were too quiet for their size.

I looked down and realized that Tark carried me across a vast sea of sand, just as I'd seen along the edges inside the medical tent. I had been transported into some kind of desert camp. He'd said the name of it... Outpost something. I couldn't remember.

Goran held back a flap of another tent—they all looked the same to me in the darkness—and Tark ducked to carry me inside and lowered me to my feet. Soft carpets were placed in a patchwork that completely covered the sand that I knew was beneath them. A bed of soft blankets and furs was on one side of the tent and a small table littered with bowls of odd-looking purple and blue fruit stood on the other.

"This is my tent for our stay at Outpost Nine. As I've discovered, you are not hurt from the transfer and easily aroused."

Tark walked me over to an odd table in the middle of the room, placed me on my feet before it, and tugged the blanket from my shoulders. My breasts swayed as I moved, the chain brushing against my belly and tugging on my nipples. They tingled from the movement and the weight.

My cheeks burned at his words and I darted a glance at Goran. The man's expression held no emotion. What did that have to do with being in his tent?

"I will fuck you now," Tark added. He spoke as if he said he'd drive me to the grocery store. This wasn't Earth and Tark most definitely didn't mince words.

My eyes widened. I tugged against his hand as I began to panic. "What? Why? We... wait! I don't want this."

He didn't release me, but his free hand began to stroke up and down my bare back. How was his touch so warm?

"As your mate, *gara*, I know your true desires. I also know and understand how to protect you here, on my world. Remember, I may not always give you what you want, but I will always give you what you need."

I didn't like his response one bit. How could he know

my true desires? We'd only just met. My pussy, however, clenched at the continuing reverberations from that medical device. Stupid dildo-shaped apparatus.

"I don't *need* to be fucked," I countered, although I didn't need to look down at my nipples to know they'd tightened at his intentions. When he'd played with my pussy with his fingers, he'd only left me more achy and aroused than ever. Unfulfilled.

He grinned at me and he looked so different, so handsome that my breath caught in my throat.

"Are you sure about that? You were dripping on my fingers just a few minutes ago. You cried out with pleasure with the neurostim exam. I licked your juices from my fingers. Would you deny this now?"

I tried to squirm away, but he was too strong. He stroked his fingers over my folds once again, then lifted them up so we could both see the glistening wetness.

My cheeks flamed.

"Your body disagrees with your mind. Obey me or you will be punished again."

I gulped at the formidable tone of his voice and still felt the sting on my bottom. "Again? But I've done nothing wrong!"

Tark sighed. "You are thinking too much. Sometimes a punishment is just what you *need*." He tugged me closer to the small table, although my feet slowed and stalled his progress.

"Obey," he repeated as he looked down at me. "Lean over the table."

I looked at the strange table, certainly not the kind that one would eat from.

"Why?" I asked, frowning.

He sighed once again, but remained calm. "Are all Earth women this contrary and curious or is it just you?"

With a hand on my upper back, he bent me over the table. His touch was gentle but the intent behind it was clear. *He would have his way, and deep down, I wanted him to.*

34

The table was narrower than I'd first thought, only covering my belly, and I hissed as the cold surface pressed to my skin. My breasts hung down and the chain dangled. I felt the table rise automatically until just my toes were on the carpet. Tark squatted down and affixed my right ankle to one table leg with a smooth leather strap, then the left to another. I tried to kick out, but it was wasted effort. The bonds were very secure.

"You may fight against the bonds, but it will do no good," Tark murmured, standing once again to push my upper body back down. His voice was hard. Bent over as I was, I tilted my head and looked up at him, but my long hair fell in the way. His eyes were so dark, so intense. His square jaw was clenched. "The claiming process must be completed so no others attempt to touch you." Tark ran his hand up and down my bare spine with gentle attention to every curve and swell. "You will be fucked. Your only decision is whether I will spank you again first."

He ran a hand over my sore bottom and I winced. It wasn't overly sore, but it was definitely a reminder that he would do as he said.

My mind latched onto something else he said. Others? Trying to touch me? Would they try to claim me, too? Was some asshole, like Bron, going to try to fuck me? I didn't like the sound of that.

Tark took my hands and placed them on small handles, and bound my wrists to the other table legs. Once I was secured to his satisfaction, he stood. I knew that my red bottom and my pussy were on display, the wetness between my legs causing a slight chill as the air glided over my naked flesh. I had never felt so vulnerable or so aroused.

I'd never been tied down during sex before, certainly not like this. The feel of the restraints that wrapped around my wrists and ankles was tight, but also oddly freeing. My mind fought everything that Tark was doing, my thoughts had been constantly tugging at me since my arrival with guilt or shame every time my body responded to him. But now, these straps set me free. Just like with the hand restraints when he'd *examined* me with that dildo thing, I could only give up, to give over control to Tark. He was going to do what he wanted—what he'd said I needed—and I could do nothing, even now, but submit. I had no decision to make, no guilt to feel for making it. No one would judge me or call me a whore if what I wanted was to be taken hard and fast. And here, now, bent over and about to be fucked by the biggest man I'd ever seen, I admitted, for the first time in my life, that being taken like this was exactly what I wanted.

Tark was my mate. Matched to me. Only to me. He'd taken away my choice, and in doing so, freed me in some strange way.

"Tark, I—"

"You will call me master."

"Master?" I frowned upside down. "Are you serious, because—"

A hard slap to my bottom had me biting back the remainder of my words. It was harder than the strikes he'd given me earlier and I cried out.

"*Gara*, feisty *gara*. A good fucking is what you need." He leaned forward and flicked the chain affixed to my nipples and set it in motion. I gasped at the delicious feel of it. "Do you accept my claim, *gara*? Do you accept my protection and my devotion?"

I hung my head. Good God. I was well and truly trapped... one last tug on my restraints had me confirming that. Tark had aroused me, tied me down, and told me blatantly and clearly that he was going to fuck me. What man had I ever met that was so direct and bossy? And why did my body like that so damn much? I wanted Tark. Only Tark. I didn't want anyone else on this crazy world. His touch, his attention, had me so hot I could barely think. He'd done a good job of arousing me, making me come, then keeping me so turned on that my brain had turned to mush, because otherwise I would have fought and yelled to be released. Instead, I waited to feel his cock fill me.

It was only for a few months until the trial. Then I'd be home, back to my normal life. Back to my boring, lonely, normal life. Back to men I knew were not matched to me, none that would be so perfectly in tune to my psychological profile. In this moment, I had a hot, virile man ready to take me, ready to give me something that I never even knew I wanted.

I lay there, my ass in the air, stinging and eager for more, and I admitted the one glaring fact—the processing center on Earth had matched me to this man, and all the arguments in the world weren't going to convince me to deny myself this pleasure. There was only one thing I could say. "Yes."

"For the official records, Evelyn Day, are you now, or have you ever been married, matched, or mated to another man?"

"No." His question slowed my thoughts.

"Do you have any biological offspring?"

"What? They already asked me…"

Another hard strike and my ass burned. "You will answer the question."

"Ta… I mean master!" I cried, trying to shift my hips. "No. I don't have any children."

"Good. Regardless of our match, I will not claim a woman who belongs to another, nor will I take her away from her children." Tark's hot palm rubbed over my ass, where my soft skin had to be a bright, brilliant pink from his firm hand. "Goran, are you prepared to witness the claiming?"

"Yes. Official recording has been activated."

I stiffened beneath Tark's warm palm. Recording? And why was Goran still here? Was there anyone else behind me that I couldn't see? The idea had me in a panic. They could see all of me and there was nothing I could do. They could see my bottom had been spanked before. It wasn't Tark who scared me, but I did not want to be shared, to be a prisoner that serviced not only my mate, but others as well.

"Tark, I don't want anyone else here."

He spanked me again, making my thighs clench. "Call me master."

"Master, please," I whispered. "Punish me if you wish, but I… I will not be a whore. I'd rather go to prison on Earth."

From my position, I could see the men's legs, but nothing else. Tark came to my side, knelt down, and brushed my long hair out of my face. "I do not know this word whore, but I understand the meaning. No, *gara*, you are mine. Only mine. No one, and I mean *no one*, will fuck you, let alone touch you, but me."

His touch was remarkably gentle on my skin. "But Goran—"

"He must witness and record us for the bride program's system monitors. That is all. They use recorded neurological reactions to assess other mates and brides for placement. It is standard protocol."

I frowned, but he said no more and rose to his feet.

As my mind tried to adapt to this new information, Tark went around behind me and stopped to stand where I could see both men's legs. I heard the sound of a belt, of pants opening just before his fingers returned to probe my core. The sight of Goran's boots barely two steps behind him made me furious. This would never have happened to me on Earth. Never.

"Standard protocol to be witnessed? To be bent over and fucked like this!" I cried. I fought against my bonds, but there was no give. I would be spanked again for this outburst, for it definitely was impertinence, but I didn't care. "Is it standard to have my nipples pierced without my permission? And what if I don't like the chain? What if I don't want to be adorned?"

As I thought, he spanked me again. The hot sting of it—he didn't hold back at all this time—had me crying out.

His voice and my position caused a memory to stir in my head, just out of reach. But when a vibration began from the table directly beneath my clit, I remembered. I'd dreamed of this, of being taken like this. Why? How had I seen this when I was on Earth? What had the processing center done to me? In my dream, I'd liked two men talking about me, touching me, fucking me. But that had been a dream.

Not a dream. Some *other woman's recorded experience.*

So, that dream in the processing center hadn't been a dream at all? I'd been reliving the stimulus and body responses of some anonymous Earth woman's claiming by her mate?

Was some other warrior going to relive this through Tark's eyes and decide he really wanted an Earth girl?

Holy shit.

Still, the processing center was one thing. I was awake now and this was *not* the same at all.

I forgot all about it when I felt his fingers sliding in and out of my pussy. "There, *gara*, that stimulator pressed against your clit should ease your mind. Remember, I will give you exactly what you need."

"And what is it that I need right now besides off this stupid table?"

He laughed, but didn't stop stroking me. "You need to come. You are dripping wet."

I shook my head. "I don't want to do this with Goran watching. You people are perverts," I vowed, gritting my teeth at the gentle, yet very deliberate touch.

Tark laughed. "Since we have been matched, Evelyn Day, you must be a pervert as well."

Me? Like this? Want this? He was wrong. "Asshole," I muttered.

"You will continue to let her speak to you in such a manner?" Goran asked, his voice sounding very surprised. Why didn't anyone argue with him?

"You can tell by the color of her beautiful ass she has been spanked for her impertinence with Bron. She has been awake and on Trion for not even twenty minutes. I am enjoying her fire and I am also enjoying seeing my handprints on her ass. She is responding now out of fear of the unknown. Even though she is aroused, her mind fights this. She is an honorable woman, not fucking just any man to quell her desires.

"For that, and that alone, I will allow it. Besides, I will revel in the lush feel of her hips, the softness of her skin." He stroked one hand down my body, grazing the side of my breast before gripping my waist. "My cock is hard for her and I will enjoy fucking my mate immensely. Evelyn Day, *gara*, you *will* like it. Fucking is never a punishment, but a reward. It is my job to see to your needs now. You belong to me."

He stroked his fingers over my inner lips, then circled my clit. He was rewarding me?

I sucked in a breath at the intense pleasure his light touch elicited. "Then… why do you have to bind me? If you're so confident in your prowess, then let me up."

His hand came down on my bottom again, then again.

"Perhaps your impertinence is because you *like* being spanked. Hmm, your arousal does slip from your pussy as I do it. Something to consider."

"What?" I cried, but stilled. He thought I *liked* being punished? That I was arguing with him because I wanted him to continue?

"I am a stranger to you, but I am your mate. It is difficult. I understand." His hand stroked over the hot skin he'd struck. It was odd, the dichotomy of his harsh spanking followed by a gentle caress. He was not a cruel man. I knew this already. "The bindings, your position, they are symbolic of our way of life, of the gift of yourself to me. This first claiming is a ritual that has existed here for hundreds of years. This is the way I must take you, and mark you as mine with my seed. It also ensures that we are compatible; however, I do not need to fuck you to know you were made for me. Your pussy is eager and my need for you is almost painful."

He bent over me next, his hard length coming into

contact with me in a very intimate way. His hard chest blanketed my back and I felt my body yield to his power, his dominance, as he whispered in my ear. "You are bound, so your body knows I am the one in control. You can let go of your fear, Evelyn Day. You are powerless to whatever I command."

He parted my folds and circled my entrance as he spoke. I cried out. I couldn't help it. There was something about his touch, as if it were electrically charged, no matter how much I fought him. It made my pussy tingle, my skin heat, my blood thicken. One finger slipped in. I could only imagine how his huge cock would feel stretching me. I wanted to see the tips of his fingers glistening with my arousal where they gripped my hips, the picture we would make with his large body covering me, his hips in place for a very thorough fucking.

And Goran watching it all, watching Tark's cock disappear inside me. Both men's gazes on me. *There.*

"Resist if you wish, but I *will* make you come." Tark stood and I bit my lip to stop the sigh of disappointment that rushed up my throat at the loss of contact.

I wanted to continue to fight, to dislike what he was doing, for I had to be some kind of slut to be aroused so brazenly by a stranger. By being watched. Bent over and bound. This ache in my pussy was impossible to rationalize. The soft hum of the vibrator on my clit proved he wanted me to have pleasure. Either Tark was remarkably skilled, or regardless to his words to the contrary, they'd given me some kind of arousal agent so I would be more susceptible to his advances.

As he slid a second finger in to join the first, I didn't really care. It was not easy to remain still. I wanted to shift my hips, to move into his touch, to take his finger even deeper. I couldn't move, though, couldn't do anything except take whatever he gave.

I didn't know this man, had only been awake for a short time, but I *wanted* another orgasm. This time by Tark

41

himself, not some weird alien body probe.

"Have you been fucked before?"

When his finger rubbed over a spot inside, I couldn't think, couldn't respond. I could only cry out. When he slipped his finger from me, leaving me empty and unfulfilled, I moaned. "*Don't stop.*"

"Then answer my question."

I shifted on my toes. "What... what was the question?"

"Have you been fucked before?" he repeated. His voice was dark and rough.

"Yes."

His fingers slid inside of me again. I groaned.

I heard the rustle of fabric, saw him step closer to me just before he pulled his fingers free and felt the nudge of his cock at my entrance. "I may not have been your first, Evelyn Day, but I am your last."

His cock was large and as he pushed forward, I felt myself widen and stretch around him. He did not relent, did not give me time to adjust, just filled me completely.

I groaned as my body felt invaded. Owned. One hand gripped my hip, the other my shoulder as he began to move. In. Out. Hard. Fast. He moved, and I bit my lip, taking whatever he gave me.

"You will come, *gara.*"

I shook my head, my hair falling down over my face. With every hard thrust, I imagined my mother's arms crossed, her brows raised in judgment. This was *so wrong.* "I just... I can't."

He leaned over me, pressing into my back, and filled me with one hard, rapid thrust. The press of his body against my sore bottom only added to the feelings coursing through my body. "I command it."

I'd never been taken like this before. My last partner had been attentive, but not overly focused. He'd left me unfulfilled and uninterested in sex. But Tark? I had no idea how he could wield his cock in such a way to rub over places inside me that I never knew existed. My fingers were slippery on the handles. I clenched my teeth as the chain between my breasts swung with every thrust.

I shook my head, frustrated. Tears filled my eyes. I was so eager, desperate even, to come. Tark was *so* good. So hard. So big. "I… I can't. I never come during… I don't know how," I cried.

Tears slipped down my temples and into my hair.

He stilled inside me, tilting his head so he whispered directly into my ear. "You've never come with a man's cock inside you?" His warm breath fanned my neck.

I shook my head. "I can't… especially knowing someone is watching."

I felt more than heard his growl, for it came from deep in his chest. "It is my job, *gara*, to pleasure you. Obviously you can find release, for you came beautifully with the medical probe."

"Yes, I can come with my vibrator, just not a man," I admitted.

Tark held himself still deep inside me. "I believe I know what a vibrator is, like the medical probe with the scans, correct? Like the stim pressed against your clit?"

I nodded my head, which made my hair swing back and forth.

"Then I will just have to discover what does it for you. As for Goran, ignore him. It is just the two of us. Shh," he crooned. "All right, *gara*, it is time to discover what pleases you."

With that, I felt the vibration on my clit speed up. The section of the table directly beneath my clit began to stimulate me in earnest. I remembered this, too, from my dream. I sucked in a deep breath at the intense pleasure the added stimulation brought about. This joining wasn't solely about Tark's pleasure, but mine as well.

"You like this vibration speed better. You are clenching my cock with your pussy," he growled. "That is a good sign, yes?"

"Yes!" I cried.

One blunt finger circled around where we were joined as Tark began to move again. The combination of his cock stroking in and out of me and the vibrations on my clit had me shifting my hips. I wanted to remain right where I was, impaled on my new mate's very large cock.

"How about this?" Tark pressed a finger against my back entrance and I stiffened, squeezing down on him again in the hopes to keep his finger out. At the same time, little pulses of intense heat and pleasure coursed through me at this dark touch.

"Relax, *gara*. Let me in. You will come when you do. I promise."

I took a deep breath and let it out, relaxing. I closed my eyes as he circled my virgin opening with his finger and slowly began to push inward, all the while continuing to shift his hips and fuck me.

The vibrations sped up, increasing the stimulation of my clit. I cried out as Tark's finger gained entry into my ass. I screamed as my entire body stiffened, every nerve ending came to life and pulsed with pleasure. Somehow, the erotic combination of Tark's cock, clit stimulation, and the tip of his finger slowly moving inside my ass set me off. I felt as if I were lost in an ocean wave, tossed and pummeled and completely out of control. The intensity of the pleasure was so much more than I'd ever felt before. Having a cock filling me to the brim only added to the orgasmic bliss that coursed through my veins. I squeezed and clenched down on him— his cock and his finger in my bottom—as if to draw them in even further.

I felt Tark's hand grip my hip as his pace increased until he thrust hard one last time, holding himself deep inside. His cock thickened, stretching me even more, just before he groaned and his hot seed filled me in pulses.

Our ragged breathing filled the room and he remained within me as I recovered. While at first it had been similar to the processing center's dream, it had not ended the same. It *wasn't* the same. I was leaving my old life behind now and forging my own way, on my new planet and with my mate.

"We are compatible," Tark said as he slowly pulled out and I heard him refasten his pants.

I hissed out a breath as he did so and I felt his hot seed drip out of me. He came around and, after releasing my bonds, he took my hand, helping me up. I leaned against the table as I gained my balance. My skin was flushed and my heart was still racing. I felt too spent from not one orgasm, but two, in the short time I'd been on Trion to try to cover myself now.

I glanced up at Tark. His skin had a flush to it as well and his eyes were softer, less intense. He looked over my naked body and his eyes narrowed and his jaw clenched as he watched his seed drip down my thighs.

"Tell the council the good news," Tark commented over his shoulder to Goran.

Reaching out, he picked up the chain that dangled between my breasts and gave it a very gentle tug. It was enough for me to move closer to him and heat to pulse between my thighs.

His eyes were on my tugged nipples as he spoke to Goran. "But first, cover her and take her to the harem."

"What?" I cried. "You will leave me naked with… *him*?" I looked to Goran in fear.

"He will keep you safe," Tark countered. "I must attend to the council meeting and you will go to the harem."

My eyes widened at his callousness, then narrowed. A harem? How many mates did this bastard have already? What number was I? Two? Four? Twenty? "You have fucked me and are done with me. I'm not a bride, I'm a fuck toy." I flicked my gaze at the other man. "I'm surprised you didn't let Goran have me, after all."

He still held the chain attached to my nipples and he wound it around his finger, forcing me come even closer if I didn't want to have my nipples tugged too much. I tilted my neck back even farther to meet his eyes. I'd gone too far in my comments, but I was afraid. If he was my mate, wasn't he supposed to watch over me and keep me safe? How was he going to do that when I was one of ten women in his life?

I'd only been on this planet for less than an hour and he was dismissing me. I wished I could contact the bride program and reject him now, but I had to wait out the thirty-day cycle or until I was called back to testify. And then? I'd make sure they knew that I wasn't happy in a harem.

He frowned. "I do not know this term *fuck toy*, but I do not think I like it. Nor do I like that you doubt my honor."

I swallowed at the deepness of his voice, the hint of anger I heard. I wanted to see the sated look on his face instead. I wanted to go back to a moment ago, when I was replete, and contemplating a future as the only beloved and well-fucked mate of Tark.

"I do not lie. I told you I do not share my mate. My seed is dripping down your thighs. My chain is prominently displayed."

His chain? Was that chain their version of a wedding ring upon my finger? Did that chain truly announce to the world that I had been claimed? Did it display his protection? What was I supposed to do? Walk around topless?

"Stimspheres, Goran." He held out his hand as Goran moved away.

He pointed at my body. "My seed and chain will ensure everyone knows you belong to me, no matter where you are in this city of tents. Your ass, I'm sure, is sore from my finger breaching you there for the first time. Your clit—" he reached down and ran a finger between my legs, "—is hard and eager for another climax. A climax only I can give you, for there will be no more medical probes or, as you call them, vibrators. Your ass is bright red from my punishment. It seems you find that all of that is not enough of a reminder that you are mine."

I wanted to move away from his surprise touch, but I couldn't without seriously hurting my nipples.

Tark twisted the gold chain attached to my breasts

around his finger even more. He lifted his other hand from my clit to take something from Goran's outstretched hand. "Leave us for a moment."

His order to Goran made my breath catch. What was he going to do to me?

Tark held up golden balls, two perfectly round spheres attached by a small chain that ran between them, and another, much longer chain with a marked golden disc attached to its terminal end.

"Clearly a spanking wasn't enough for you to learn to curb your disrespect and sharp tongue. You are going to carry these stimspheres until I return for you. The chain must be clearly visible at all times, *gara*, so that all who see you know that I am displeased."

My heart fluttered faster than a hummingbird's wings and all I could do was stare. Carry around a couple of golden balls? *That* was punishment?

His gaze never leaving mine, and his grip around the twisted chain holding me in place, he lowered his hand to my wet pussy and inserted first one, then both of the golden spheres deep inside me. When he dropped his hand, the spheres slipped past my inner muscles and back toward his palm. He held his hand there, unmoving, as he stared into my stunned face. "You will hold these inside your pussy, *gara*, until I return for you. Or you will be spanked again. This time I will not hold back and you will not be able to sit for a week."

Holy shit, he was serious. And the entire situation made my pussy clench. His seed slipped from me, but not the balls. Just that fast, I was eager for him again.

Tark smiled at my wetness and his seed that coated his palm, lowered his head to kiss my neck, and shoved the spheres back up inside my pussy as his tongue traced hot lines over my collarbone. He lifted his head and removed both of his hands from my body at the same time.

When he let go, the longer chain I had seen swung down between my thighs. The weight made the chain heavier, but each swing of it sent a small electric shock to my clit.

I gasped as I clenched down on the weighty metal objects.

"The spheres will keep you aroused, *gara*, but the neuroprogramming will not allow you to come. Making you come is my job, and my job alone." He traced the curve of my cheek with gentle fingers and stared down into my eyes. "If you remove it, I will know. The stimspheres are linked to my monitoring system." He pointed at a device he had strapped to his forearm.

"Once Goran uploads the data from your claiming, everyone in the interstellar coalition will know you have accepted the high councilor's claim, that you belong to me. With that," he indicated the spinning golden disc that hung between my thighs, "perhaps *you* will remember the same and temper your tongue."

He lifted me from my feet for a brief moment to make sure the disc was swinging. I hissed out a breath at the feel of the jolt of stimulation inside my pussy and I clenched down hard. A mixture of discomfort and desire made me shiver with every pendulum-like swing of the golden chain as I watched him leave the tent. I was thoroughly chastised, naked, well fucked, and swiftly returning to full arousal.

CHAPTER FOUR

The pixel image sent with Evelyn Day's profile information was a horrible representation of the stunning beauty I'd just fucked. In the image, harsh lighting had cast a purplish glow to her skin, her hair—a true fiery red—had been matted and appeared dark. The soft strands were anything but. They curled wildly, were soft and shiny and the color of the blood moon. In the image, her eyes had been wide with what I had imagined to be fear and her mouth had been pinched in a flat line. The vibrant and feisty woman who'd arrived to the remote transport station was nothing like her official profile image, and that fact pleased me immensely.

When she'd first awakened, her eyes met mine first. *Mine.* Bron had been a *fark*, eager to get his hands on her under the guise of medicine. He'd even had a cock stand for my mate. His job with me was over and he would get nowhere near Evelyn Day. The unethical *fark* would be lucky to get a position on a transfer trawler headed for deep space.

I couldn't believe that Evelyn Day had been selected from billions of potential mates to be well and truly mine. I had barely been able to wait through the examination—*fark,* that process had only made my need worse—to see my seed coat her creamy white thighs. Perhaps my eagerness was one of an overly randy youth, but I'd waited so long for her.

But now, I feared the long wait had made me not only eager, but too kind. My mate was a criminal convicted of murder. Even Goran had questioned my actions when witnessing how I'd been with her. My mate was a killer. But when I looked into her eyes, watched every tick of her pulse, held awareness of her every breath and tasted her lush body's response to my touch, I could not keep that one simple fact in my mind.

Evelyn Day. Twenty-eight. Convicted of murder.

The Interstellar Bride Program had sent her name, age, those three words, and a pixel image. Nothing else.

Who had she killed, and why? I was a warrior and I knew the cost of taking a life. I had done it many times. Some men deserved to die, but others were simply following orders, or fighting for the wrong side. Some fought to defend their homes or their mates. Others relished the taste of life and death on their tongue.

Evelyn Day did not have the eyes of a woman who enjoyed killing. She was soft and warm. Giving herself to me had made her pussy hot enough to scald my cock. Such sweet agony.

Murderer or not, there was no chance she could harm me. I almost laughed aloud at the idea. I was unfamiliar with the men from Earth, but she was too small to be a danger to me; her head only came up to my shoulder. She'd been feisty and disrespectful, but I could not blame her actions. She had just been banished from her planet and was now the mate of a stranger. That did not mean her behavior went unchecked. She'd needed a spanking to learn right away that her insolent behavior would not be tolerated. After I'd tossed her over my thighs and gave her the swats she deserved—albeit lighter than I would once she settled in— she knew who was in charge and who would submit.

Seeing the pale globes of her ass change from creamy

white to fiery red had made my cock rock hard. Watching the soft flesh quiver with each strike, seeing my handprint form... *fark*. I was not the only one who'd enjoyed it. She would certainly argue, but she'd been aroused by it. The testing matched her submissiveness to my need for control. It would only be a matter of time before she recognized this and relented.

Until then... it would be enjoyable to watch her fight, then ultimately give over to me. With a satisfied grin, I checked my monitors and set the stimspheres I'd left inside her pussy to the lowest setting for two hours. I planned to be done with my meeting in half that time, and I wanted her pussy swollen and eager for more. I couldn't wait to get her home, safe, where I could lay her down and taste her, take my time and explore every inch of her creamy skin. I hadn't even been at Outpost Nine a week, but I was ready to get back to the palace. Now, more than ever.

I'd offered Evelyn Day no opportunity to transition, no chance to acclimate to either me or Outpost Nine, for there had not been time. It wasn't just my cock dictating my actions, Trion custom did as well. I'd had to fuck her immediately. If I hadn't, another could have claimed her. Her beauty would not go unnoticed here. Women were precious and rare, highly valued. Many would fight to claim her, and it was possible she could be hurt or claimed by a male completely unworthy. When it came to Evelyn Day, *I* was the only worthy man in the universe. I growled in possessiveness at the idea.

She wore my adornment, the chain adding beauty to her full breasts and signifying her as mine. With my seed marking her pussy and thighs, there would be no doubt. Her safety was my utmost priority. Her arrival had been a shock, the timing all wrong, but I wasn't going to complain. The match occurring while I was at the high council meeting at Outpost Nine, not at the palace, might be inconvenient for both of us, but I would adapt. Keeping her safe could prove difficult here, but it would be done.

I couldn't bring myself to regret that Evelyn Day had her first fucking over a ceremonial stand in a transient tent, not in my palace chambers, where she wouldn't have had to leave my bed. Instead of learning all of her delights and beginning her training to my ways, I'd had to send her to the harem to ensure she was well protected. And that caution was well founded.

Once the other men saw her, they would want her as well. Her bright red hair was a most unusual color, rarely seen on Trion. Her body was lush and had the most delightful curves. Such passion in one so small, so soft, so delectably round and curvy. I pushed the button to the bathing unit with more force than necessary at the thought of her full breasts swaying with every movement of her body.

The unit's door opened and I stepped in, allowing the water to spray and swirl around me. With my eyes closed, I thought about her curved belly, the softly rounded body that would soon grow with my child. Hips broad and lush for holding as I fucked her.

The water shut off and the drying cycle began.

I was pleased she had already been breached, for I did not have to worry about causing her pain. But I'd been delighted—and surprised—to discover that the walls of her pussy had never pulsed around another man's thick cock, that no other had managed to bring her to that pleasure. Those she'd been with on Earth were not real men if they could not make a woman of Evelyn Day's beauty come all over their cock. It would be my ultimate goal in life to bring her to pleasure as frequently as possible.

I didn't know if I should thank the gods or science for the perfect matching. Either way, I had no doubt Evelyn Day was for me. She, however, had time to decide. Therefore, I had to heed a fine balance between pleasuring her into remaining and taming her reckless and possibly dangerous behavior. The thought of her choosing another, of letting another man touch her, fuck her, protect and cherish her, made my gut clench.

I dressed quickly, then walked to the tent for the general council meeting. I pushed away my anger and frustration at all the possible political implications of my new mate and savored the lingering feelings of satisfaction I'd found in her body. Many on the council made no secret of the fact that they wanted to assume my role and take the mantle of power from my shoulders. The idea that one of them might attempt to use Evelyn Day as a pawn in a coup made me clench my hands into tight fists.

Perhaps my mood—angry and surly—was better than that of a satisfied lover for this meeting of the general council. For now, I knew that my mate was in the harem, that she, along with the other women, were safe. Only when we returned to the palace and she was protected, by not only the thick walls but the full contingency of my loyal guards, would I breathe easily. I could not even allow her to sleep with me, as I desired, for fear of being attacked in the night by those who wished to take my place.

"She is safe," Goran said as he approached, his footsteps muffled in the sand. I turned to my second-in-command and nodded. With the knowledge that Evelyn Day was under the eyes of the well-trained guards, I could focus on the business at hand. I opened the tent flap, ducked and entered. The general council stood in deference to my rank as high councilor among them.

"Be seated," I said, moving to the raised dais and lowering to a pillow, as did the others before me.

"We have heard your mate has arrived." Councilor Roark grinned at me and I nodded my head. He was young and not yet mated. As councilor of the southern continent, he was my closest ally among this group, but also the most virile of the men. Evelyn Day would tempt him greatly.

"Yes, and she has been claimed." I lifted my chin at Goran, who stepped forward from his place, standing along the perimeter of the meeting circle.

"High Councilor Tark's mate has arrived. She passed her

medical examinations and has been claimed per our protocols. All data have already been sent to the Interstellar Bride Program for processing." He stated the facts in a voice that invited no argument or dissent and I was grateful. Goran was loyal. A good man, and one waiting for his own mate to arrive. He would fight beside me, even die with me to keep Evelyn Day safe.

"Very well. Thank you, General Goran." Councilor Roark nodded gravely and I realized that he had acted in my best interests, ensuring that my mate's status was clear to all present. I tipped my head to him in acknowledgement and thanks.

"A criminal. A killer? And this is the type of female you expect us to obey? To respect above all others?" Councilor Bertok was a bitter old man who had lost two mates already. He was ninety years old if a day, and his pale blue gaze never failed to be cold and unfeeling. "We could all be killed in our sleep. A rugged woman from the wildlands would be a better match than a convict from another planet."

"I have accepted my mate. Claimed her. There will be no more discussion." I wanted to pummel the old man into a pile of mush with my bare fists, wanted to feel the hot splash of his blood on my skin. "No one threatens my mate and lives." I glared at each man around the circle to make sure they understood the sincerity of my words.

"Understandable, high councilor. Perhaps a public beating. You must show your strength and let your mate know who is in control." I ignored the councilor to my left and his eager suggestion. No one would see Evelyn's pain but me, and even then it would be tied to her pleasure.

I eyed the man carefully. He meant no disrespect and was not threatening Evelyn Day directly; on some parts of the planet, a public beating was a way for a man to show his domination over his woman. The idea was barbaric and something I was trying to have outlawed.

"When will the public claiming occur?" Another voice, this time from the opposite side of the circle.

The comments and opinions continued... and escalated. It reached a volume and intensity where I'd had enough. I raised my hand and silence fell. As ruler, I found it important to hear the opinions and thoughts of the councilors. I never wanted those I ruled to feel that they had no say. Before today, their voices had been used for planetary business. Even though I was the high councilor, my personal life and my mate were not up for discussion.

"As is custom, and as my second-in-command has said, she has had her first fucking." I tilted my head to Goran who sat off to the side and nodded his confirmation once again. "The act has been witnessed, recorded, and reported." My hand fisted at my side and I wished for a blade to twist my fingers around. None of these men would see my mate's personal pleasure. I would not share. Ever.

"We should have all been present." Councilor Bertok spoke again. He was from the outer region, the wildlands he had mentioned, and I knew their customs regarding their mates was much more brute strength than gentle persuasion. While I knew the first fucking must be witnessed, it did not mean I enjoyed the idea of providing pompous *farks* like him with sensual entertainment at my mate's expense. My life as leader was under constant scrutiny, but there would be one aspect that would remain private. Once back at the palace, my actions with my mate would be ours alone. Not even Goran would be in attendance. I would train her to my personal expectations, not to those of the entire council.

I did not respond to the comment, but said, "I have claimed her. She is marked by my seed and she bears my chain. There will be no further discussion." I curled my fingers, beckoning Goran to join me. "If you look at the agenda for this session, we can start with the economic gains made in sector four."

I turned my attention to the reason for this meeting. Continuing to talk about my mate only extended the time I would be kept away from her. Her life on Earth—or what she'd done to be banished—did not concern me. She was here with *me* now and I would not let her go.

• • • • • • •

"Look at the chain dangling between her legs. She hasn't pleased him." The woman's shrill voice had me spinning around, the chain whipping against my thigh as I did so. I hissed out a breath and picked up the chain to hold it so it would stop stimulating the walls of my pussy. That didn't work. I had only been carrying the spheres in my body for a few minutes and I was ready to weep and beg Tark for relief from the constant pleasure. It was a subtle hum, enough to constantly remind me of his control over me— and my orgasms—but not enough to bring me that sweet release.

They vibrated and pulsed similarly to the medical probe, although in a much more subtle way. By having to hold them inside, I had to clench my inner walls, which only added to the delicious torture.

Several women stood before me. They all wore an identical simple garment that looked like a sheer slip dress. I could see the outline of nipple rings through the thin material, but I couldn't see that any of them had a chain strung between them, as I did.

The woman who'd spoken was beautiful, except for the sneer on her lips. Her dark hair flowed long down her back. She was tall and willowy with small breasts and a slim waist. She was everything I was not.

The skin on my bottom was sore and I wondered if they could see the marks Tark's touch had left on me through the thin slip Goran had given me to wear. My complexion was pale enough that I couldn't even hide a simple blush. A red bottom would be blatant. Their scrutiny was intense, eyeing me as if I'd come from a different planet—which I had.

"I am Kiri," one of the women said as she stepped

forward. She was shorter than the annoying one and while curiosity laced her expression, there was no malice. With a tilt of her head, she added, "The others are Lin, Vana, Ria, and Mara."

I didn't know who was who, so I nodded at all of them.

"We were working on our craft when you came in. Please, join us."

The space was similar to Tark's, with carpet covering the ground. Similar lights made the room have a soft yellow glow. The air was warm and the scent of almonds filled the air. I recognized the aroma from my dream at the processing center.

She turned, along with the others and settled at a table where they seemed to be carving small pieces of wood. There were several comfortable chairs, a low coffee table— God, did they have coffee here?—and another tall table against one wall that was laden with various platters of food and pitchers of various colored liquids. While I associated a harem as a type of prison, there were guards outside after all, the amenities matched that of Tark's own tent.

The ladies settled in to their tasks, all except for the thin, beautiful one. She stared at me as if I'd been brought in with the trash.

"He will reject you," she snapped.

"Mara, leave her be," Kiri said.

Mara rolled her eyes at the other woman's words, but only I could see the disgust and envy on her face. "I hear only convicts are sent from Earth. What was your crime?"

I had no friend in Mara, that much was obvious. Perhaps a little fear might go a long way instead, so I told her the truth. "Murder."

The other women stopped their work and one hissed in pain. "Ah, I sliced my finger."

She held her injured hand in her other one as the women circled to tend to her.

"I can help." I attempted to step around Mara, my medical training urging my body forward before I stopped to consider.

Mara gave me a push on the shoulder. "Help? By killing her, too?"

I paused and watched as a small device was waved over the wound. A blue glow was emitted and, over the next few moments, the wound stopped bleeding and healed before my eyes.

While I was a doctor on Earth, it seemed that the medical advances on Trion were far superior. My scientific mind found it fascinating. "That is amazing. You are completely healed?"

The woman cleaned the blood from her hands with a damp cloth offered by one of the others, then held up the now healed finger. She smiled and nodded. There was so much to learn and I was eager to examine the healing tool.

Mara took my arm and walked me—none too gently— across the tent so that none of the others could hear her foul words. "He's fucked all of us, you know."

When I frowned, she smiled, then continued.

"You don't know? Hmm. Tark fucks all the women. You are nothing special to him. He could call on any one of us to please him, anytime he wishes. His choice."

She looked down at me, raking her eyes over my plump body with disdain.

"Then why was I sent here and matched to him?" I asked, tilting up my chin. I wouldn't let her see that she'd upset me. The idea of Tark being with Mara, or any other woman—no, *all the other women*—made my belly churn.

"Because he needs an heir. Look at you. Overfed, ample hips, drooping bosom. You were made for birthing. Now I—" she tossed her hair back, "—was made for desire."

The tent flap opened and one of the guards stuck his head in, looked around. "Mara, come at once. He wants you now."

My mouth fell open and her eyes lit with triumph. She rolled back her shoulders and plucked at her nipples through her slip until they were tight points, the rings clearly defined. "See?" she called with a backward glance, then left, the tent flap closing with a slap behind her. I stood and stared after her, feeling hollowed out and empty, with two spheres inside my pussy and holding the attached chain in my hand like a dog holding its own leash. Even the vibrations that they emitted did nothing for me any longer.

I'd only been off-planet for perhaps an hour or two but I'd been fucked and found wanting by my own mate. Mara had stated Tark was only interested in me for breeding— why would he want curvy old me for anything else?—and he had called for her to slake his insatiable lust just minutes after he'd watched his seed slide down my thighs. I was just one of many in the harem. I wasn't desirable, I was just the plump girl who could birth babies.

So, here I was, destined to be nothing more than a breeding machine, forever treated like a criminal? A murderer? I wasn't much on Earth, but even there I was more than this. An innocent medical doctor with no love life? Yes. But I healed people, I didn't kill them.

Now, here on this sandy planet, I was nothing but a baby factory. A biological machine. But me, the woman? The bride? The healer? *I* was worthless.

"Where do I sleep?" I asked Kiri. I could hear the dejection in my voice. She lifted her head and gave me a sympathetic smile.

"Through there." She pointed to an opening in the tent I hadn't noticed before. Ducking through, it was a secondary tent, the two connected.

Within were piles of soft woven blankets and furs on raised platforms, similar to beds. There was another table laden with a basket of breads and fruit and a drinking flask filled with a clear liquid that I assumed was water. One look at the food and my stomach rolled.

I found a small space where the blankets were folded and appeared unclaimed. I climbed up, pulled the warm covers over me, situated my new leash so the stimulation to my core might stop, and rolled onto my side to face the soft-sided wall.

I shifted carefully, afraid I'd catch the other chain and pull at my nipples, but once settled, I became attuned to other parts of my body. I was wet between my legs, Tark's seed still seeped from me. I was sore inside, for while I never saw his cock, I knew it had been big. Too big for my barely used body, and now stuffed with metal balls he'd called stimspheres. Then there was my ass. I was sore there, too, for nothing had ever been placed inside, not even a tip of a finger. My bottom stung from his punishment, a glowing heat that hopefully would dissipate soon. My body was still soft and pliant from the orgasms Tark had wrung from me. The fact that I'd responded so readily only made my misery greater.

How could one man bring me both mind-blowing pleasure and heartbreaking disappointment? He'd called for Mara after he'd sent me off to the harem. A harem! God, I was just one of many for the man. He'd said I was his mate, that I belonged to him, but he did not belong to me. Was that the custom here? How could any psychological profile or assessment have identified me as the type of woman who would be happy as one of many women in a single man's bed? There had to be some kind of mistake.

Not that it mattered. I needed to keep my head about me. There was much I would be forced to endure over the next few weeks, but I also needed to remember that once the trial started, I would be transported back to testify, to return to my life on Earth. Tark would be on the other side of the galaxy. Mara, the bitch, would be on the other side of the galaxy. I just had to survive in the meantime. The prosecutor had said that the trial was scheduled to take place in three months, but the date was never guaranteed.

At least I couldn't get pregnant before Earth's criminal justice system sent for me. Thank God. What would happen if I got pregnant before I went home? What would I do with Tark's child growing in my womb back on Earth? Thankfully, as part of the witness protection program, I had an implant that would prevent pregnancy. Someday, I'd have it removed. But not here. Not now. I wasn't a baby machine.

I shuddered beneath the blankets. I was trapped here for a few weeks. Maybe three months. In the meantime, what would happen to me? I was weary, exhausted, and the spheres inside me continued to pulse. I reached between my legs to rub my clit. He'd said they would make me aroused, but not enough to come. Suddenly angry at my predicament, I wanted to test his word, to discover if his claims about the device were true. Besides, I wanted to relieve the ache between my thighs, to sink into mindless pleasure for the length of an orgasm. I circled my clit with the flats of my fingers. I was slick and wet. Tark's seed was plentiful.

Pressing my heels into the bed, I shifted my hips. I knew just how to make myself come, I'd done it often enough. This time though, I thought about Tark, saw his face in my mind, pretended the vibrating spheres deep inside me were his cock. It was enough to make me gasp in pleasure, make my inner walls clench and squeeze. I worked my clit for several long minutes before I caught my breath and slumped, the spheres continuing to hum. But, as Tark had promised, the programming prevented me from reaching orgasm. I was sticky and sweaty, aroused and completely unfulfilled.

Unfortunately, the added stress of need on my body did nothing to help my weariness. Surely the ache in my chest had been caused by the transfer, and not by a sense of betrayal. I did not care about the man who had claimed me. Fucked me. Used me and abandoned me to these cackling women. The only punishment the gold spheres had provided was humiliation in front of Mara, and now, a deep and painful ache in my core, an ache that longed to be filled. An ache that reminded me that I was nothing to Tark but a machine he planned to use to produce heirs. And Mara? The vile woman was probably coming all over Tark's cock right now, spread-eagled and tied to that small table, calling him master as he took her from behind.

The image hurt, and it shouldn't have. Tark was nothing to me. I'd known him a couple of hours. I had to be reasonable. Logical. I tried to distract myself by concentrating on thoughts of home. Walks in the park. Coffee and chocolate. My warm bed in my nice, comfortable apartment.

I would be home soon enough. I just had to survive this until then, and remember that Tark wasn't going to be mine. Not really. Not forever.

Sure, Mara was a bitch. Tark was deceiving. I didn't know what to think anymore, nor did I care. I just wanted to escape the only way I could, so I gave in and let sleep take me.

CHAPTER FIVE

"She refuses," Goran said, rising to his full height after coming into my tent.

I turned and my eyes widened. Had I heard him correctly? "Refuses?"

He seemed nervous as he nodded, for no one refused me. Until now.

"Did she give a reason for this disobedience?" I could hear the anger in my voice, but I was calm. Was it the Earth way to defy, or just Evelyn Day's? Was this her attempt to reject me? Too late for that. She was mine. If she'd suffered a change of heart since her very satisfying fucking, then it was up to me to sway her. Perhaps my punishment had been too severe for her human mind? Was it her diminutive size? I needed to discover what Evelyn Day needed to be happy, and if her bliss would come through punishment or pleasure.

"She did not."

"She is still with the harem?"

He nodded again.

I stood and went out into the warm air, Goran holding the tent flap open for me. I nodded in greeting to those I passed, but perhaps it was the intent look on my face that kept them from speaking to me.

The guards at the entrance to the harem stood at attention at my arrival. I ducked into the women's tent. Several women rose and greeted me.

"Where is my mate?" I asked. While two of the women jumped at the sharp tone of my voice, I did not give them much attention. I did not focus on others' mates. Now, I solely had interest in my own.

One woman pointed toward the secondary room.

There, I found Evelyn Day sitting upon a bed brushing her hair. She looked calm and peaceful, completely unsurprised by my appearance.

"You will come when I send for you," I said.

She looked up at me and I saw fire in her eyes. Shrugging her shoulders, she put the brush down and began braiding the long length into a single plait. She waited to speak until she tied off her braid. "I'm surprised it matters so much to you, for any one of us is as good as another, right?"

She stood and she was lovelier than I remembered. She wore a slip like the others, but the thin material was snug on her body and did not hide any of her curves. Her hard nipples and the rings that adorned them were clearly outlined, the chain a soft curve beneath the fabric. The material was taut over her wide hips and only fell to mid-thigh. And there, dangling between her thighs was the proof of my will. I had deactivated the stimspheres hours ago. Perhaps she needed another reminder of who was in charge, or perhaps those spheres had been what pushed her too far into defiance. Either way, she was more alluring now than when she was naked.

Her body distracted me and I had to remember her question. I frowned. "Any one of us?"

"The women in the harem."

"I don't know to what you speak. Do men on Earth share their mates with others?"

"This is a harem, isn't it?"

"Yes."

Her mouth fell open slightly, then she narrowed her eyes. "There are no harems on Earth, not anymore. They haven't existed for centuries. This is *your* harem, isn't it?"

"This is the harem for all at Outpost Nine," I replied.

We stood before each other and I was completely unused to this kind of conversation. People usually listened as I spoke, then replied with a very sincere, "Yes, sir."

I was not used to the sheer quantity of her questions. I doubted I would soon get a 'sir' past her lips, let alone a 'master,' at least not while she had clothing to cover her soft skin.

She was quick, for I barely saw her pick up the brush and toss it at me. I almost didn't move out of the way of the hard object. *Fark*, she had excellent aim!

"You plan to share me with the entire outpost?" She hissed the accusation, her voice filled with venom and pain. The look on her face was one of rage, but behind the fire in her eyes was the pain of betrayal. "I told you I'd rather go to prison on Earth than be a whore."

After my surprise passed, I rolled my shoulders back and glared down at her quivering form. "And I told you I share you with no one."

The volume of my own voice had her taking a small retreating step, but she tilted her chin up. She was so defiant, and that fire made my cock hard as a rock. I wanted to taste that fire, use my mouth on her until she whimpered and begged me to fuck her mindless!

"Yet, I am forced to share you with the others?" She crossed her arms over her chest, which pushed the upper swells of her breasts up above the slip.

I gritted my teeth at the sight, for my cock was hard and my hand twitched to spank her ass for her insolence. She caused frustration to tighten my chest and my fists clenched at my sides. *Fark!* My mate was supposed to be biddable and sweet, not a woman who would hiss at me or question everything I did. But I would not take her or touch her in anger.

"I have no others," I replied.

"Ha!" She laughed without any humor. Clearly, she did not believe me. Why? Why would she consider my words to be false?

Lifting a hand, she waved about the room. "Then what is this?"

I looked around the space, opulent even for an outpost. "It is where the women are kept for their safety."

Out of the corner of my eye, I saw the flap between the two rooms shift and I knew we were not alone in our conversation. I sighed. No doubt the other women had overheard our disagreement, and I did not need my personal life to be the subject of their gossip or fodder for those who wished to overthrow me.

Bending forward, I placed my shoulder at Evelyn Day's waist and tossed her over it, careful of the chain I knew dangled beneath her slip. Clamping a hand at the back of her thighs, I ducked and entered the other room, the women stepping back to let me pass.

"What are you doing? Let me down!" Evelyn Day muttered, her small hands pounding on my back.

As I spanked her ass, I realized her shift had crept up and I tugged it down to cover her. If I was going to carry her across the outpost, I didn't want everyone to see her pussy and delectable ass.

She had been misled about something relating to the harem and was furious about it. I had to resolve this, for I wanted to sink into her again, to mate with her, feel her beneath me, make sure she knew she was mine. But until this confusion was resolved, I would most assuredly be denied.

"We are going to my tent. While the harem will keep you safe, it will not allow us any amount of privacy. For what I plan to do with you, privacy most certainly is in order. I would like to speak to you without raising the attention of the entire outpost, therefore you should hold your tongue."

· · · · · · ·

Before the harem's tent flap closed behind us, I caught a glimpse of Mara's wicked smile. I knew her smirk wasn't born of friendship. Most likely, she greatly enjoyed the knowledge that I would be punished. Based on the way the other women deferred to Tark, I had to assume most didn't defy him as I did.

The way his eyes had widened as my hairbrush bounced off the tent wall, I had to assume he'd never had anything hurled at his head before, either. I hadn't been able to help it. The man made me so mad! How dare he lean over me, his cock filling me completely, and whisper in my ear that I was his, then, only a short time later, request Mara to come to him?

If he found that vile woman appealing—though I had to admit her body was what most men desired, even if her personality was certainly lacking—then I wanted nothing to do with him. Surely the processing center's matching program had made a very large error.

The processing center's machine had delved into my mind, seeking the best match based on subliminal, subconscious wants and desires. In the chair, I'd dreamt of being taken by a man while another watched. Their words had been base but sexy—hell, even downright carnal—but I still had to question if that was what I really wanted. I'd been adamant about Goran not touching me, and thankfully Tark had proven to be just as particular, at least up until now.

Surely even my subconscious mind didn't want a man who sought the comfort of others.

I felt the warm air on my skin as Tark carried me across the outpost. It had been dark the last time I'd been outside. A full day had passed, and once more the light of day had faded. Inky blackness surrounded us, and on top of that, I was upside down. My mate was not giving me much opportunity to glimpse my new world.

Quickly enough, we were inside once again and I was lowered from Tark's shoulder. He was slow about it, and when he set me upon my feet on the carpeted ground, he looked me over with an assessing gaze as if to assure my well-being.

We were in Tark's tent.

"Where's the fucking table?" I asked. "Do you expect me to bend over it again? Is that how Mara likes it? Or is tying a woman down the only way you men on Trion can fuck a woman?"

Tark stood quietly and let me toss out those barbed words. He wore attire similar to the previous day. Black pants, gray shirt, although this one had short sleeves and was a pullover, with buttons down the front. His broad shoulders and chest were well defined beneath the trim fabric. He was so big and yet he was the most perfect specimen of a man I'd ever seen. They didn't make men like this on Earth, at least I'd never seen one. His dark hair was a little tousled, perhaps from carrying my heavy weight about.

It was his eyes, though, that were so expressive. I saw a glint of anger there, but he was remarkably calm. Calmer than I was. His gaze also held surprise and definitely heat.

"Are all women on Earth so difficult?"

"Do all men on Trion fuck everything with a pussy?" I countered, my voice shrill.

Instead of yelling, he knelt in front of me. Before I could figure out his intent, he had reached under my thin gown and removed the stimspheres from my body with a gentle tug on the dangling chain.

I gasped as they slid out and my pussy felt empty. I clenched down and it felt odd to have them gone, even though they'd stopped vibrating sometime while I'd been asleep. He set them aside, forgotten on the carpet.

"It seems that I will have to come up with alternate forms of punishment, for my device appears to have made both your mouth and your temper worse, not better." I opened my mouth to speak, but the look he gave me had me remaining silent. "We barely know each other, and today I will remedy that." Tark came to his feet, so close that the heat of his chest reached me across the narrow space. "You are questioning my honor, but I find that your anger pleases me."

That was not what I expected him to say. I expected him to yell and wave his arms around and perhaps even toss me over some fucking stand and spank my ass again. But please him? He'd stunned me into stillness.

"It... it pleases you?" I asked.

"Yes." He grinned and wrapped his strong hands around my upper arms just tight enough that I felt treasured, but not threatened. He knew how to disarm me. Damn the man, he was even more handsome when he grinned and my heart rate kicked up a notch. Just seeing him smile could be bad for my health. "You believe that I have done something dishonorable and you are upset about it. It pleases me that you would demand honor in your mate."

I had no retort for that.

"I wish to know what dishonor you would lay at my feet."

"You are well aware of your actions. Or perhaps there is a short-term memory problem here on Trion?"

Tark released my arms and I covered them with my own hands instantly in a sorry attempt to hold in his heat. He moved to a chair, sat down and leaned back, stretching his long legs out before him. Placing his elbows on the armrests, he put his hands together. "I have a perfect memory, mate. Now, tell me what displeases you."

I sighed. Perhaps all men, no matter which planet they were born on, were obtuse.

"Did you forget that you'd just fucked me when you sent for another?"

His eyebrow arched then. "I requested another woman? Who?"

While Mara didn't like me, I didn't want to get her

angrier. I felt like I was tattling like a child, but Mara hadn't gone off in search of Tark, she'd been requested. I was only stating fact.

"Mara."

Tark frowned. "Now your earlier statement about Mara makes sense. But Mara belongs to Davish, and I assure you, even if she did not, she would not be a woman I would request."

It was my turn to frown. I was starting to feel a little uncomfortable, as my anger was quickly falling away. My insecurities were beginning to show. I looked down at the patterned rug.

"Oh." I replayed the scene from memory. The harem guard had not mentioned Tark when he told Mara to go. Just *he*. That *he* had obviously been her mate, Davish.

What a bitch.

Through my lashes I saw him shake his head slowly. "I sent for the woman I wanted, and she refused me."

My head came up then. He crooked his finger, beckoning me closer. I swallowed as I stepped toward him, the rug soft beneath my bare feet.

"Do men on Earth claim any woman they want?"

I shook my head. "No."

"Do men on Earth have no honor?"

Tark put his hands on my hips and pulled me to stand between his parted knees. The hot feel of his grasp made me gasp.

I shrugged. "Some do not."

"I assume you have only had interactions with the dishonorable sort?"

I looked at his forearms, thick and corded with muscle, covered with dark hair.

"Some."

"Are you familiar with what a harem is?" he asked.

I glanced up at him, his dark eyes clear and focused on me. The anger was gone, from both of us.

"They had them on Earth a long time ago. Certain

70

cultures allowed a man to have several—many—women just for himself. A harem was the name used to include all of his women, but also it could be the place where they remained until called upon to service his needs."

"I now see the problem we have." His thumbs stroked up and down the top of my thighs, working the thin material of my slip higher and higher until he stroked over bare skin.

"A harem on Trion is a place, well-guarded and fortified, where a woman stays when a man cannot offer protection. Each of the women you met belongs to someone, just as Mara belongs to Davish and you—" he leaned forward and placed a kiss on my abdomen, "—belong to me."

The way he said *you belong to me* caused a little brightness of hope to flare to life. "I thought—"

"I know what you thought. I've told you my name, but I did not tell you that I am high councilor. I am sure there is a similar role on Earth, perhaps with a different title. I am the leader of the northern continent and the seven armies. We are here at Outpost Nine for the annual general meeting of the planet's other councilors. Each of us represents a different region or area of the planet."

"We have something similar on earth, but each country has a leader. There is not a leader for all of Earth."

"And are all countries equal on your world? Or do some hold more power than others?"

"There are a few large countries that control almost everything."

"That is how it is here as well. My region is the most powerful and the largest. Do you now understand the importance of my role and the danger that follows both me and my mate? Yesterday, I wished to shield you from all the curiosity."

I bit my lip. "Curiosity?"

"Politics would demand that I select a woman from Trion as my mate, but I refused many offers. I waited for an interstellar bride because I did not want a political match. I wanted someone who would be mine, and mine alone, with no political agenda and no ulterior motives. I wanted a woman who would be a perfect match for me, the man. As you are."

I tilted my head, but all the fear, all the worry was gone. "How can you be so sure?"

"I knew the moment the transfer was complete."

He seemed so sure of himself, that we'd been matched across all the possibilities in the galaxy. I hadn't even intended to be matched. I *should* be on Earth, in the hospital treating patients. He believed I would remain here on Trion forever, but our match was short term, only until I was called back to testify. Suddenly, the idea of leaving didn't seem as promising as it should have.

His hands shifted and cupped my bottom, pulling me closer.

"Then... then you promise me you didn't send for Mara?"

I heard him growl deep in his chest. "Woman, I wouldn't have requested an interstellar bride if I had wanted to fuck Mara."

He must have seen something on my face, for he added, "Have I eased your mind? Are we of similar understanding now?"

I bit my lip and let the tension and worry I'd been feeling seep away. "You sent me to the harem to keep me safe?"

"I had a meeting with the councilors and I could not watch over you. I protected you with the harem guards when I could not be with you."

I smiled then. It was a little wobbly, but it was there. "I'm sorry. I am not used to a man choosing me over a woman like... like Mara."

"Now I am the one confused. Why would any man choose Mara over you?"

I huffed out a laugh. "Perky breasts. A flat stomach. Narrow hips. Thighs that aren't dimpled with cellulite. Hair that is smooth and tamed."

Tark's eyes narrowed and he silently worked the slip up

and over my head, tossing the garment to the carpet. The chain brushed my belly as it swung.

"Your punishment is getting longer and longer."

"What?" I tried to step back, but his iron grip prevented it.

"Tossing a hairbrush at your master is most definitely a punishable offense. Behaving like a shrew in front of others calls for stern retribution. Speaking about yourself with negativity is even worse. I will not hear you speaking about yourself in such a way again."

"But—"

He swiftly turned me, then pushed me down and over his lap so I was once again in position for a spanking. His palm struck my bare bottom.

I reached back to cover myself, but he grabbed that wrist and held it securely. God, he'd done that the day before and I should have learned. I should have learned many things, but I was once again bottom high in the air.

He spoke as his palm rained down. Unlike yesterday, this spanking was much harder, the strikes hitting everywhere with an intensity that had me up on my toes and struggling in his tight hold.

"I like my woman to have curves. I like my woman to have hips I can grip as I fuck her."

I couldn't help the cries that escaped my lips. It hurt! This wasn't a simple lesson on my behavior; this was an all-out punishment. "I like my woman to have breasts that are a handful." His hand stroked over the heated skin. "How can you question this?"

I tried to catch my breath as he paused. "Because I'm short and fat."

His spanking began again and I scrunched up my face at the searing pain and fought against his grip on my wrist. "*Gara*, how were you assessed for our match?"

His hand reached around and a thumb flicked over a gold ring. I sucked in a breath at the pleasure that elicited. Combined with the harsh sting of my bottom, my pussy clenched. My clit ached to be touched and I felt my thighs grow damp.

"They attached sensors and gave me something to trick my mind with visions. They made me look at hundreds of images. Then I slipped into a dream. When I woke, the match was done."

Another round of spanking began, this time he shifted the strikes to hit the tops of my thighs. As he pushed them apart, the blows landed on the tender skin and I couldn't hold back the tears any longer.

"I submitted to something similar. You are exactly as I want because my subconscious says so. Just as I am exactly what you want."

As I sobbed, I thought about his words. My subconscious chose him. I hadn't considered, until this very moment, that his had chosen me in return. A perfect match. Everything he wanted and desired in a lover and a mate. The idea that I was as physically perfect in his eyes as he was in mine? I couldn't wrap my head around it. How could I be perfect if he had to keep spanking me?

Slowly and gently, he lifted me up and placed me before him. Using his thumbs, he wiped the tears from my cheeks. When my eyes cleared, I saw his dark eyes held tenderness "Enough talk. You were a good girl and took your punishment well. It is time to fuck my mate."

CHAPTER SIX

Tugging me forward, he pulled me onto his lap so I straddled him, my knees on either side of his thighs, taking care that my sore bottom didn't get bumped.

Even through his clothing, his body radiated heat. This was the closest I'd been to him. Sure, he'd been deep inside me, but I hadn't been able to see him, to look in his dark eyes, to see the desire there. He was giving me the opportunity to study him. Up close, I saw his nose had a slight crook in it, as if it had been broken at some point. With the odd medical device that had been used on the injured woman's hand, it should have been easily fixed to perfection. Instead, he looked *imperfect*. He had full lips and I wondered what they would feel like against mine.

I doubted he would be a gentle kisser, but be as dominant with his mouth as with everything else. As I continued to think about him kissing me, he groaned, deep in his throat.

"That look, *gara*. It is my undoing."

My gaze lifted to meet his. Between my parted legs I felt his cock, a rigid length that pressed against my pussy. If his pants weren't in the way, surely he'd only need to shift his hips and he would be deep inside me.

"Do you... kiss?" He hadn't kissed me, not once. He'd fucked me, made me scream, spanked me, and explored my body with his hands. But a kiss? I wanted to know how he tasted.

His dark brow arched and the corner of his mouth tipped up. A dimple formed in his cheek, almost hidden in the dark stubble. God, he was so handsome and he was mine. I couldn't feel any more aroused if I tried. Surely his pants were soaked through because my pussy was dripping on them. Could he feel the heat from my bottom on his thighs?

I barely knew anything about Tark and he knew nothing of me, and what he did know was a lie. But elementally, we didn't even need to be more than strangers, for I wanted him with an intensity I'd never known, never felt before. I was like the druggies who came into the hospital, strung out and desperate for another fix. My body craved his. I wanted another hit of the pleasure only he could give me. His scent was almost taunting, the feel of his taut muscles, the way he looked at me. I couldn't question the validity of the match. The match was real. This attraction was real.

But I wouldn't be staying here. When it was time to testify, I would return to Earth and he would be countless light-years away. I would be returning to a world where there was no one for me. No one as *right* as Tark.

I had about three months. While I would be leaving, that didn't mean I couldn't take advantage of all Tark had to offer—even if that meant punishment.

"Kiss?" Tark asked. He frowned for a moment. "Of course. You don't?"

I darted a look to the side, then back at him. "Yes, but you've never kissed me, so I wasn't sure."

He sighed. "As I said, we are at Outpost Nine for the councilor meetings, which conflicts greatly with my desire to be with you. I am not free to devote myself to your pleasure, to learn your body the way I will once we return to the palace. Do you think I wish to be with a bunch of cranky and very opinionated men when I could be like this with you?"

His hands moved to my hips and stroked over them. The movement nudged my clit onto his cock and I moaned. The heat of the action was intense.

"I am coming to like that sound you make," he murmured.

His eyes were on my mouth and I licked my lips.

His grip tightened as he watched the innocent action. He liked it. I did it again and he groaned.

"You are a bad girl."

Before I could utter a reply, he leaned forward and claimed my mouth. For a man so big, so powerful and dominant in nature, the kiss was soft, gentle. For a few seconds, then it changed. It turned wickedly carnal as his lips claimed mine and his tongue delved deep as I gasped in surprise. He tasted like wine and decadent, dark male.

He could kiss. Boy, could he ever. It was like lighting fire with gasoline, instant explosion. Bright and hot and scorching in intensity. I'd been kissed before, but not like this. I'd been touched before, but Tark's hands were so large that I felt contained, possessed, claimed. And he was only touching me with his hands and mouth. What would it be like when his cock wasn't constrained in his pants but stretching me open, filling me up?

I reached up and cupped his head, afraid that if I didn't hold onto him in some way, he might disappear. It was like the dream, the feel of him. This time, I was awake.

"I'm not... I'm not a bad girl," I gasped, then let him claim my lips again.

After an interminable amount of time, he pulled his head back and looked at me, his eyes half lidded and dark as midnight. His lips were shiny from my kisses and his breathing was as ragged as mine. Power shot through me that I could do this to him, make him be this... insentient.

"Murder." He only said the one word, but it was enough to remind me that, to him, I was a *very* bad girl.

"But—" I wanted to tell him the truth, that that was a lie, but he covered my lips with his fingers.

"Beauty. Fiery spirit. The most perfect pussy. Moans of pleasure. You wield your powers well."

I couldn't help but smile at his words.

"My power, *gara*, is over your pleasure. You may not come until I command."

That shouldn't be much of a problem, for I couldn't come for a man. Well, I couldn't come for a man before him.

"Tark—"

"Master." His hands moved to lift the chain that dangled between us, twirled it around his finger to shorten it and force me closer until our lips touched. "You will call me master, for while your power has turned my cock as big and hard as a *trundle*'s horn, you will do as I say when it comes to fucking."

His words, while lust-filled, were still clearly meant as a command.

"I'm the only one who can give you your pleasure, aren't I?" he asked.

He tugged gently on the chain and I hissed out a breath as the painful pleasure jolted straight to my clit. How did he know I liked that?

"Yes… master."

His eyes widened at the word from my lips. Calling him master hadn't been as terrible as I'd expected. I was a doctor. I was an independent woman who considered no man her master. But when I said it in reference to Tark, it was different. He was most assuredly the master of my body, and I was content with that for now.

"Ah, perhaps you are a good girl after all. Let's see about that. No coming, *gara*. Not until I command it."

With one last tug, he let the chain go and reached between us to stroke over my pussy.

"So hot, so wet. Put your hands behind your head. Yes, like that. Now keep them there."

I intertwined my fingers behind my neck, my elbows sticking out. This position also had my breasts thrust outward. He seemed to enjoy having me bound, but on his lap as I was, there was nothing to use to tie me. Forcing me to hold this position was like having invisible bonds and I clenched my inner walls at the thought. I could do nothing but what Tark bid.

He played with me for a bit, his fingers slipping over my folds, dipping inside and stroking—oh, God!—my G spot. He didn't linger, but moved to circle my clit, tormenting me by not actually touching it, only building me up and up until I was about to come before pulling his hand away. Again and again he did that. I moved my hips into his hand, but every time I did so, he stopped. Then started again. Groaning, I remained still, briefly, until I couldn't hold back any longer. My fingers started to slip, but with one arch of his dark brow, I tightened them against my neck. It was a cycle of complete torture and the look on Tark's face—smug satisfaction—let me know his dominance was complete.

Every cell in my body screamed for release, and that was just from his skilled hands. I would surely die once he actually fucked me.

"Master, please," I begged. My skin was slick with sweat, my throat dry, my nipples tight little pebbles, and my clit throbbed. Every part of my pussy ached for Tark's cock.

Placing his hands back on my hips, he murmured, "Take out my cock."

Lowering my hands, I eagerly did as he bid, sliding back on his thighs so I could reach between us and open his pants. Did all men from Trion not wear underwear or was it just him? His cock sprang free, tall and erect and pre-cum seeped from the tip. My eyes widened at the sight.

While I'd felt his cock as he'd fucked me the day before, I hadn't seen it. I'd never seen one so big. It extended thick and a dark, ruddy red from a nest of dark hair. Bulging veins pulsed up the long length. A broad, flared crown capped it.

That had fit inside of me?

I grasped the base of it firmly—my hand didn't even close about it—and slid up, using my thumb to swipe away his visible sign of eagerness. I licked my lips, wondering what he tasted like. Salty? Musky? Surely pure, unadulterated male.

"Keep looking at me that way and I'll come in your mouth, not your pussy." He voice was deep and rough, as if his control was barely leashed. "Put me inside you."

His hands lifted me so that I hovered over him, placing me exactly where he wanted me. Still gripping his cock, I lowered myself so that the head pushed against my entrance. As I continued to lower myself further, he began to stretch me open, to fill me more and more.

I put my hands on his shoulders for balance and gripped him tightly once I sat upon his lap completely. He was fully seated within me, the flared head nudging the entrance to my womb. I felt filled, stretched, and completely claimed. The heat and sting in my body only accentuated that.

I sighed, reveling in the feel, for I felt... complete. My pussy clenched around him, little shockwaves of pleasure rolled through me. The stimspheres he'd inserted only made me more sensitive, more aware of every place he stroked.

Tark's eyes fell closed and his teeth ground together. "*Fark*," he hissed, just before he gripped my hips and began raising and lowering me.

I tried to shift, to rub my clit against him every time he lowered me down, but his hold was too secure. All I could do was feel as he rocked his hips up in counterpoint to him lowering me.

My breasts bounced and made the chain shift, my nipples tingling and tight, the weight adding to the sensations coursing through my veins, but it was not enough to get me to come. How did this man know how to get me so close to the edge and not push me over? It had never been this intense before. Our skin was slick with sweat, our breathing rough and ragged. Wet sounds of fucking filled the space and I could hear myself cry out in pleasure, only increased by the painful counterpoint of my sore bottom rubbing against his thighs. The rest of the outpost was just outside the flimsy walls and could no doubt hear—and know—what we were doing. I didn't care. I only cared about being with Tark and letting him rule my body. No wonder I'd never come for another man.

"We will come together, *gara*," he growled and I swear I felt him grow even bigger inside of me.

He reached between us and flicked over my clit, all the time his dark eyes held mine.

I couldn't keep them open, but his voice stirred me. "No, look at me. I want to watch your face as you come, as you take my seed."

My inner walls clenched down at his words, and I came. My eyes widened, almost in surprise that I could feel this way, that this man could give it to me. I cried out, the sound escaping my lips. I couldn't hold back. I couldn't hold anything back. As I arched my back and ground down on his thighs, riding out the pleasure, I watched Tark as he clenched his jaw. His cheeks flushed and he growled. The tendons in his neck tightened and I felt his cock pulse, his seed filling me. I knew my pussy was gripping him like a fist and almost pulling the cum from his body, as if it needed it, craved it.

Spent, I slumped forward, my head resting against Tark's shoulder, our chests pressed together. My pussy continued to clench and squeeze in little aftershocks and I had no desire to move. The way Tark stroked his big hand up and down my slick back, neither did he.

I didn't know how long we remained like this, but Tark stood, keeping himself deeply embedded as he walked across the tent and laid me down on my back as he loomed over me. He held his weight off of me with his forearm. A thick lock of hair fell over his forehead and I swiped it back, although it just fell back in place.

"Evelyn Day, you please me."

"Eva," I replied.

He frowned.

"I go by Eva." It was important to me that he called me by my real name, not the false one given by the prosecutors for my secret identity. That wasn't me. Nothing about Evelyn Day, the murderer, was me.

"Eva," he repeated, as if trying out the name. "What is it that you do on Earth?"

He frowned even more, the furrow in his brow deepening. "Why do you roll your eyes at me?"

"You want to have a conversation like this?" Tark was lying on top of me, buried to the hilt, covering me like a heated blanket. His face was inches from mine, hovering and focused on me with such intensity that I was finding it hard to focus. I'd never felt so consumed. So treasured. So intimately linked to another person.

He stroked a hand over my hair and I resisted the urge to nuzzle into the strong warmth of his palm. "What, with my cock still inside you?"

I nodded against the soft mattress.

He grinned and my heart melted a little. "Nothing will get between us, *gara*. Besides, I want to ensure my seed stays inside and takes root."

"You... you want a baby?" The men I knew were not interested in babies at all. "I have an implant against conceiving."

He shook his head. "As part of the processing, that was removed. Remember the probe?" How could I forget? "It confirmed you are fertile and capable of being bred. You do not wish for a child?"

I shrugged and looked at the crisp hairs on his chest, ran my fingers over them. They were silky soft and I could feel the beating of his heart beneath my fingertips.

"I do, but on Earth, I had no man. I assumed I would have children someday. You have had longer to consider," I added.

"I have. It is a requirement that I produce an heir."

I stiffened beneath him, not pleased to be considered just a vessel for his progeny.

"Do not get riled, Eva. I also want to have a child, a little girl that looks just like you, red hair and all. Perhaps a little less spirit, for if she will be anything like her mother, she will be the death of me."

I grinned up at him at his playful barb. I couldn't help but be pleased by his words.

"Don't you need a boy to carry on the line or something?"

He shook his head as he stroked a finger over my shoulder and watched as he raised goose bumps. I could feel them break out across my skin.

"No. It matters not."

His nipple was a flat disk, a shade darker than the rest of his skin and I slid my palm over it. He placed his hand on top of mine and my eyes lifted to his.

"What... what was the question?" I'd been distracted.

"What did you do on Earth? Surely murderer was not your profession."

I stiffened beneath him, my knees pressing into his hips. "I was... I am a doctor."

One dark brow winged up. "Like Bron?"

"I do not know his specialty, but I believe so. I practiced emergency medicine."

"Impressive," he said.

"From what I've seen, Trion may be more advanced than Earth. You seem to have quite an array of useful tools."

"Ah, you mean the probe?"

I swallowed, remembering how that dildo device had made me feel. "I assure you, we have nothing like that on Earth. If we did, the emergency room would be overrun."

Tark grinned.

It seemed he was intent on having a conversation and did not plan on pulling his cock from me. "Were you born as high councilor or elected?"

"The position became mine at the death of my father. I

will pass the role on to my first child."

"A monarchy then."

"Yes. Monarchy." He tried out the word. "As I told you, there are others who wish to overthrow me, to rule in a different way. Many are used to harsher customs and wish to see them installed in all regions. I have a more... flexible approach that I hope allows for diversity in customs across the planet."

Besides an amazing lover, he was a leader and a diplomat.

"Being mated to a murderer probably doesn't help you." Surely he'd come across some who would dislike me based on my false past.

He made a noncommittal sound as he reached down and slid his hand along the chain between my breasts.

"Do you plan to murder me?" His eyes followed his fingers.

"No." I sucked in a breath when he started to gently tug the chain so it pulled on one nipple ring, then the other. "Don't you want to know what I did?"

"You will tell me in your own time. For now," he shifted his hips ever so slightly and I felt him move inside me. His seed eased his passage. "Again," he murmured, as he moved his hips.

My eyes widened as I felt how hard he was—had he ever gone down?—and how I was just as eager.

His cum slipped out around his motions and dripped down between my legs and onto the blankets beneath me.

"Master," I whispered as he pulled out a little further, then slid back in. He was bigger than the probe he'd used on me. Hotter. He was more adept at wielding his cock and my body responded.

He grinned, clearly pleased by the single word, and took us both up and over once more.

CHAPTER SEVEN

Two more days passed; my time filled with meetings forced me to send Eva to the harem so that I was assured of her safety. Besides being beautiful, she was a reasonable woman and understood why I could not keep her with me. A spanking had certainly helped with that. Because of this, I did not have another hairbrush tossed at my head.

It wasn't Eva who was complaining, it was the other councilors. I sat at my usual seat above the others and listened to them grumble.

"We did not witness the first fucking and we have not laid eyes on her. Only mates in the harem can confirm her existence." Councilor Bertok was a continued nuisance.

"Councilor Tark is not at home. Surely you can understand his need to protect his mate," Roark replied.

"From whom?" the old man asked. "She's the murderer. It is we who should be fearful that she won't harm one of the other women in the harem." He lifted his arm up to indicate the others. "Aren't you concerned for your mates? The guards are protecting the women from *external* dangers, but perhaps the real danger stays *within*."

"Enough," I said.

All heads swiveled toward me.

"Goran, bring my mate to me."

My second-in-command nodded once before leaving the tent.

Talk returned to the latest agenda topic until Goran returned. He held the tent flap open as Eva entered. I stood and the others followed. Holding out my hand, she came to my side. She was lovely and every man in the room only had eyes for her. Fortunately, she was dressed in her plain slip dress and wore a robe over it, long enough to swirl about her ankles. It had no buttons or closures, but Eva held the two sides together in front of her chest.

I gave her a small smile—I could not give her more, for if the councilors knew of my deep-seated interest in her, it may prove dangerous. We were both under scrutiny.

I leaned forward and murmured in her ear, "Some of the men are more formal and stricter in their customs than others. Please, defer to me."

While I could see some confusion in her light eyes, she nodded and remained silent. I hoped, for her sake, she would not question me. I did not wish to spank her publicly.

"This is Evelyn Day, my mate."

The men all stared at the woman to whom I'd been matched.

"As you can see, she is too small to be a danger."

I saw her look at me out of the corner of my eye.

"She could be hiding a weapon," Councilor Bertok said, eyeing her with disdain.

I rolled my shoulders back. "You question my mate?"

"Have *you* questioned your mate? She has committed a heinous crime on her world. The only punishment she received was to be sent here. Surely Trion is a more advanced and improved world than Earth. How is arriving here enough of a punishment?"

Councilor Bertok needed to retire, for his ways were too archaic. Unfortunately, he didn't have to play diplomat. I did. What he said was also true. I had yet to ask Eva the details behind her actions. Cold-blooded murder was a grave offense on Trion. Was it so on Earth? What *had* she done? I would ask her, but I would do it in private. Later.

"Evelyn Day's crime and punishment were the responsibilities of her world, not ours. She is here as my mate, nothing more. If she is to be punished, it will be because of an infraction here on Trion and I will see to it as her mate."

The old man stood. "I will not remain while she is free."

"What do you expect me to do, Councilor Bertok, imprison my mate, the woman sent to me by the Interstellar Bride Program? Would you turn your back on the treaty that keeps all of Trion and hundreds of other worlds safe because you are afraid of a woman? You are the one who wished to see her."

"She should be kept in chains so our women remain safe. If not, we should all leave."

Two other councilors also stood and nodded their agreement.

I couldn't have the men leave. I needed their presence to close out the meetings, for I did not wish to return to Outpost Nine again for another year. And yet I refused to see my mate shackled just for their enjoyment. Discipline was required—when needed—but I was not going to punish Eva solely because of one man's whim. I would punish Eva when the occasion required, spanking her until she submitted to my hand, but not now, not when she'd done nothing to earn it.

The man was pushing his power onto me via my mate and that was unacceptable. He knew I had to do as he bid. Inwardly, I wanted to rip the man's head off and place it on a pike, but outwardly, I called for Goran.

"Bring me one of the luminaries."

Goran probably questioned my request, but remained silent and did as I bid.

Turning to Eva, I said, "Kneel."

She narrowed her eyes, but complied. Glancing up at me through her lashes, a very carnal image of her in just such a position as she sucked my cock came to mind. Fortunately, Goran returned.

"Remove the light," I told him, and he removed the glowing portion from the top. I took the pole from him. "Thank you."

He nodded and retreated.

"Lift the chain from beneath your dress," I told Eva.

She looked first to the men, then at me. I saw fire in her eyes and for a moment I thought she would disobey, but fortunately, she remained silent and did as I bid again. She lifted the chain from between her breasts and let it hang on the outside of her slip dress. Perhaps, and I would like to hope, her quick response was based on a growing trust between us. I'd said more than once I'd never hurt her and I'd proven that by only touching her in pleasure. Spanking her ass, not once but twice, had been painful to start, but I knew from the way her pussy had been wet, she had liked it. Perhaps it was a poor punishment for someone who liked a hint of pain. Something to consider. Later.

I knelt down and carefully fed the bottom of the pole through the gap between the chain and her body and jabbed it into the ground, watched as it sank and secured itself into the sand. I tugged on it to ensure that it was well placed.

The pole was placed within the circle of the chain and her body. Eva was not going anywhere, unless she decided to shimmy up the long pole to unhook her chain. I doubted she wished to rip her nipple rings from her body. This arrangement allowed her to be confined, yet completely unbound. She was by my side—and modestly covered— where I wanted her and I could easily release her if danger came upon us. A swift yank on the pole and she'd be free.

"Satisfied?" I asked Councilor Bertok.

He pursed his thin lips, but nodded and returned to his seat. He could do nothing else and he knew it. I'd met his requirement, although he had most likely expected me to strip her bare and shackle her in chains. The old *fark*.

The crisis was averted and yet the cost was solely heaped

upon Eva. She kept her head down throughout the remainder of the meeting. She was, no doubt, embarrassed and very angry. While I focused on the agenda at hand, I monitored Eva carefully, assessing she was comfortable. While I was high councilor, I was also her mate and she was my top priority. I had committed myself to my role my entire life. It was time to commit myself to Eva.

As I brought the meeting to a close, one of the head guards ducked into the tent. By the urgency on his face, the sweat that dripped from his brow, something was wrong.

"High councilor, there has been an accident. Several are dead and we have injuries."

• • • • • • •

It was possible I'd been more embarrassed when Goran had watched Tark fuck me, but it had been eased by arousal and ultimately an amazing orgasm. Being forced to sit on the raised platform beside Tark, not as his equal, but clearly as his... woman, or worse, a chained pet, was beyond mortifying. While he hadn't actually tied me up, handcuffed me, or shackled me as that awful Bertok had wanted, I had been truly trapped. The chain attached to the nipple rings had kept me by the pole just the same. Tark was being considerate, but I was bound nonetheless. I'd fumed over it for the first few minutes of the meeting, but then realized my mate was doing his job.

Variation in custom occurred across Trion as well and Tark had to meet these differences of the councilors. Instead of shackling me, he'd devised a way for me to subjugate myself while providing me some dignity. I knew Tark's strength and he could easily remove the pole from the sand as quickly as he'd placed it.

It had been the look in the men's eyes that kept my head lowered, that made me feel inferior, not Tark. I didn't want to see the leers, the arousal, the eagerness, even the curiosity that I'd seen when I first came into the tent. I only wanted

Tark's gaze on me. I liked it when I saw his eyes flare with heat. I liked knowing he was eager for me, that his curiosity rivaled mine for him. I didn't mind any of it with Tark because I'd brought that about and I felt powerful, not slutty.

Was this what he had been trying to prevent by keeping me in seclusion? I'd hated the feeling of being hidden, kept from everyone else around me. I wasn't used to it, but now I knew why. Outpost Nine was... uncomfortable, even for Tark. He'd had to make accommodations of his personal beliefs, his customs and convictions with the other councilors—it was obvious now with Bertok and a few of his followers—and I would have to compromise with mine. I'd been outspoken and he had spanked me to teach me the laws of the land. I was fortunate I'd been chastised before now, for I had learned to hold my tongue. If I hadn't, surely Tark would have been forced to spank me in front of the entire council. His position not only as my mate, but as high councilor, would demand it. He'd talked about the palace, the city where he lived. Fortunately, our stay in this encampment was temporary.

But when the guard came in sharing the news of an accident, I didn't want to keep my head down or remain hidden. I wanted to do my job.

Tark stood immediately and yanked the pole from the sand, releasing me from my pseudo-confinement. I jumped to my feet. Tark grabbed my arm and dragged me toward Goran.

"Take her to the harem."

As Goran nodded, I said, "No! I might be able to help."

The room had broken out into pandemonium. Everyone was talking at once, many leaving the tent with guards surrounding them.

"You mean your medical training?" Tark asked, his voice pitched low so only Goran and I could hear.

I nodded. "Besides, we don't know if the accident was truly that or some kind of attack."

Tark's jaw clenched, but he was considering. He hadn't said no yet. I didn't want to be sent back to the harem, twiddling my thumbs and idly letting the world pass me by. Someone might die if I didn't help and that went against everything inside of me.

"Consider that it could be a distraction to steer everyone from the harem," I added. "You must admit there are many who do not like me. Hurting me means hurting you."

Tark didn't like my comments, but I could see he knew them to be a very distinct possibility.

"Please, Tark," I begged. "I am of more value to this planet, to you as high councilor, to you as a mate than just a breeder. You may think me a murderer, but I am skilled at what I do. Let me help."

He took another moment to decide. "Very well. You will stay beside me at all times. You must obey, Eva. Do you understand?"

"I do."

My heart leapt into my throat as I realized he was going to allow me to join him. He was trusting me, allowing me to be more than what was normally expected of a mate. I could not sit idly and make woodcraft and he knew it. The matching, God, it was incredible, for Tark knew deep down things about me that other men would never see or take time to discover.

"Extra guards. Now," Tark commanded to the men outside the tent. "Follow us."

Tark gripped my arm and followed the man who'd interrupted the meeting. Goran followed closely on my heels. We weaved through people agitated from the news. As we walked, I was able to observe more of Outpost Nine than I had before. I'd been correct in my assumption. All of the men were large. Only a few women were about, all accompanied by a male escort. I looked down a long line of tents and saw stalls similar to a bazaar or fair at the far end. Smoke wafted and scents of cooking meat, almonds, and strange spices permeated the air. As we walked, I became winded, my skin beading with sweat. The sun was intense, but I did not wish to block my view with the robe's hood.

"What has happened?" Tark asked the guard.

The man looked back, his face grim.

"Davish and his contingency were headed toward the leader's section to the south when they were raided. They'd only gone part of the way when the attack occurred. Those who survived turned back, knowing the best chance for aid was here. The sentinels saw their return and called for help."

"Drovers?" Tark asked.

"Most likely. They are long gone, but a squadron was sent to hunt for them."

The differences between Tark as a lover and as high councilor were impressive. While he was dominant and commanding with me, his touch, his voice, even the thrusting of his cock, while deliberate, were quite gentle. I never feared him. Now, though, looking at the tense lines of his shoulders, the awareness of power about him, made him almost a different person. His guard was up, his defenses ready for whatever we would face.

We came out from between two tents and the land opened up. Looking left and right, the outer edge of the outpost was visible, made up of a long line of identical temporary structures. It was a vast town in the middle of nowhere, if the vista before me was any indication. I'd been to the desert southwest with a friend from college one holiday break. The landscape was arid and scrappy. There were no trees as I'd been used to where I'd grown up outside of the country's capital. The sky in Arizona was big and blue, the rock formations orange-red. That was the only desert I'd seen, the only thing I could compare this to. But the desert here, on Trion, was completely different from anything I'd ever seen before.

The sand was white, like the beach, an endless ocean that went on for miles and miles in every direction. Scrubby purple, red, and brown plants dotted the rolling landscape and a few jagged gray rock formations broke up the straight horizon. What made me gasp were the two moons I could see in the sky, one white and one blood red. Holding my hand up over my eyes against the glare, I just stared. But not for long.

The guard pointed and to our right was a small group of people and large animals. I thought immediately they must be like camels, since we were in the desert, but they actually looked more like longhaired horses. Men held the leads for the animals, who had been placed in a protective circle surrounding people who lay sprawled across the ground. Tark pushed his way into the center and tugged me with him.

I counted quickly, my training kicking in. The familiar adrenaline pumped through my veins. Eight people lying on the ground, men and women both. Some thrashed about, clearly injured and in pain, others lay still. One was obviously dead from where I stood, brain matter seeping from a crack in his skull.

One of the men saw our arrival, stood from beside an injured woman and closed the distance between us swiftly.

"High councilor." He nodded in respect. "We have one dead, three on their way to death, and the remainder have injuries that are not life-threatening. Unfortunately, our probes and scanners can't fix the severity of some wounds."

"Something's wrong. She's bleeding profusely!"

We turned toward the shout. Another man knelt before the injured woman. "It just started and I can't get it to stop. The ReGen wand doesn't work!" He was panicking, his eyes wide as he watched the blood pump from the wound in her thigh. The man waved a small device over it, but there was no blue light this time, and I noticed no improvement.

"That's an arterial bleed. I have to help."

A hand on my arm stopped me.

I looked up at Tark. "You can spank me all you wish later, but I need to help. Now. She will be dead in a minute if it's not stopped." I tugged at the grip.

"The severe cases can be taken to the med unit," Tark

said.

"They will die before they arrive and there are no revitalization pods," the man countered. Had he even seen an arterial bleed before?

"*Fark*," Tark whispered.

I yanked even harder at Tark's hold as I watched the blood begin to soak into the sand beneath the injured person. "I can help, you idiot mate. I'm a fucking doctor. It's my *job* to help."

"You?" the other man asked, stunned.

Either Tark loosened his grip or I'd been able to break free. I didn't respond to the man's remark, but instead said, "She needs a tourniquet immediately." I dropped to my knees in the sand assessing the injury. I didn't look up when I called out, "Find me some simple pliers and a needle and thread."

The three men paused briefly.

"Now!" I shouted.

"Get her what she needs," Tark commanded and they moved to do his bidding.

I grabbed the long hem of my robe and tore a strip from the bottom. Pushing it beneath her leg, I wrapped it around her thigh above the large gash, blood spurting from it. How she'd survived since the attack, I had no idea. My only thought was the woman had been injured further in rough transit. Yanking on the strip, I made a tight knot above the cut, the blood flow tapering off.

"Her femoral artery has been nicked. Perhaps moving her made it worse and it tore." It didn't matter how it happened, it just had to be fixed. I was thankful for the short length of the customary slip dress she wore, this time the lower half covered in blood. The robe on top was similar to mine, but did not cover her, instead was spread out beneath her on the ground.

I stuck my fingers into the gash and quickly found the nicked spot. "Get me the pliers." I looked up and Tark was above me, shielding my eyes from the sun. He was a dark silhouette above me, but I knew it was he. "Pliers," I repeated. "Some kind of clamp or a way to hold the artery closed while I sew up the hole."

Before he could move, the man who'd met us came running up and handed me something similar to pliers. "This should work well." With slippery fingers, I clamped off the artery. "I need someone to hold them."

Tark knelt beside me, our shoulders bumping, and held them in place. "Keep them closed."

"Needle and thread?" I asked.

It appeared to my left, the needle already threaded and ready to go. Leaning forward, I carefully and methodically sewed up the small hole. It only took a few stitches, but those small knots were the difference between life and death.

"Release the clamp, but don't remove it. I need you to be ready to put pressure on once again if the sutures don't hold."

Tark loosened his grip on the clamp and we watched as the stitches held. I knew men stood above us, but I was not interested in them, only that the woman's artery would hold.

"Can she be repaired with that... wand thing in the med unit?" I asked, my hands directly above the gash, ready to add more sutures if need be.

"Yes, now that the blood has stopped."

I didn't know who spoke, but he stood to my left.

"Use the ReGen Wand on her here before you try to move her. Get as much healing done as you can so there's no chance it will open again. Only when the artery itself is repaired can you remove the tourniquet. But be quick, or she'll lose her leg." I waved my bloody hand in the air. "Either heal that artery, or be very, very careful when you take her to the pod thing you talked about."

Several men took my place beside the patient. It was only then that I saw her face—that I paid attention to something besides the dire wound—and recognized Mara. I was covered to my forearms in her blood. I was glad to see she would make it. She might have been a total bitch, but that didn't mean she deserved to die.

I turned away from her since she was stable and being tended. "The patients have been triaged, so who is next?" I glanced up to wait for the answer. When no one responded, I looked at the other wounded. "Who will die if they aren't treated immediately?"

A hand pointed behind me and I spun about and tended to the next patient. I didn't know how long I worked, but it took some time to stabilize a man that had a punctured lung. Using a simple sheet of a plastic-like substance that was attached to a strange electronic clipboard, I was able to create a makeshift seal for the wound to allow the man to breathe better. Stabilized, he was led to the med unit for the ReGen wand. I didn't know what a revitalization pod was, but it sounded like something I'd like to check out.

The remainder of the injured had been carried off on simple pallets to the med unit. I braced a broken leg, but Trion's gadgetry could heal it better than me making a cast, which I couldn't do in the middle of a desert, no matter how good my skills.

When the last of the wounded were gone, Tark approached, along with a few other men. I must have been a sight. I had blood up to my elbows, my robe was torn at the hem and hanging off my shoulders, and smears of blood coated the front of my slip dress. I was sweating and my hair clung to my damp forehead and neck.

I was tired and hot and hungry and the adrenaline had worn off, leaving me in no mood to be led back to the harem or tied to a stake or told I was a murderer. My hackles were raised when the man who'd met us spoke.

"I am Doctor Rahm. That was quite impressive."

I lifted my head to the man in surprise.

"High Councilor Tark told me that you were a doctor on Earth. Watching you work was incredible. Your field skills are far beyond any medical technician here on Trion and I am thankful you were here today to help. I fear we have become too dependent on our technology. Thank you for assisting us today."

I cleared my throat, for it was so dry and I was quite thirsty. "Thank you."

"I have heard that the first of the wounded have completely recovered in the med unit, the others are almost complete with their revitalization. Even the woman with the leg wound."

I couldn't help but smile, knowing that my skills had been helpful, that people had lived because of me.

"That is good to hear."

The man eyed me with curiosity, but not like the men on the council.

"I would like to talk to you further, for perhaps you can teach some of us your skills. The knot work you did on the sutures—"

"Doctor Rahm, my mate is obviously weary." Tark's protective voice cut the man off. "You may question her another time. She needs a bathing unit and food, otherwise she will need revitalization of her own."

He bowed slightly. "Of course. I apologize. I have not seen someone of her skill here on Trion."

"I will arrange a time for you to meet, if that is acceptable to you, Eva."

Tark was deferring to me, which was a surprise in itself. He was the one who had been in control in our relationship. I was the one who submitted. This change was a surprise.

"Yes, of course."

"Until then, thank you." The man bowed, not to Tark, but to me, and retreated.

Tark leaned down so he could whisper in my ear. "It seems, *gara*, that I am not the only one enthralled with you."

CHAPTER EIGHT

I was in complete awe of my mate. Once back in my tent, I helped her strip off her bloody clothes, letting them fall to a dirty pile at her feet. I thought of her as she'd helped the injured people. The way she'd deftly saved Mara's life had been scary and exhilarating and intense.

A ReGen wand hadn't been able to tackle a wound of that size. They were made to treat small cuts and scrapes, injuries that didn't require full use of the regeneration units. Doctor Rahm hadn't been able to help Mara. People on Trion didn't die very often from the kind of wound Mara had. We had healing tools that resolved most emergencies swiftly and efficiently. In this particular case, combining the remote location and other factors, the tools were ineffective. Skills that Eva had were what had been needed, what our doctors needed to learn. Waving medical devices about only did so much. Perhaps this was a topic for the high council. If Eva's hands-on skills could save a person on Trion from death, then they were worth teaching our medical technicians.

I opened the bathing pod door for Eva and set the unit to run the full cleaning cycle. "Remember to close your eyes," I murmured, remembering the first time she'd used the machine and hadn't known what to do. It had been a scary experience for her. She'd told me how she bathed on Earth and while it was archaic, the idea of having my soapy hands on her naked body had made my cock hard. "The blood will come off and you will be cleaned without any scrubbing."

This time, she was much more docile, a combination of familiarity and weariness.

I'd been to battle many times and remembered the feel of the tension in the air. The high stakes. It was life or death and the rush of adrenaline in my blood had me almost high for hours after. Then, it would wear away and I'd be drained, as if my energy was washed off me in the bathing unit.

While Eva had not gone through battle—she'd been perfectly safe with me and the guards surrounding her—she had a similar reaction. She'd tended to everyone else and now it was my turn to tend to her.

Once finished, she stepped out and not a hint of blood remained. Her beauty was breathtaking. Her mind, her intelligence was awe-inspiring. I was more amazed by my mate than ever before.

"Stand still, *gara*."

Reaching up to my chain, I carefully undid the links that attached it to the nipple rings, one side then the other.

She watched me, then looked up and frowned. "Why are you doing that? Are you… giving me back?" Fear blanched all color from her cheeks.

"Oh, *gara*, no." I stroked my finger over that soft, pale skin. "I want to adorn you in another way. You have pleased me today. Made me see you… me… things in a new way."

I took her hand and led her to my bed, had her sit in the middle upon the blankets and furs. Lifting the lid on my small chest that sat beside the bed, I pulled out the gems and held them up.

"I am not sure of the custom on Earth, but a man on Trion adorns his mate with jewels."

She nodded. "On Earth, it's usually a ring."

I looked at her unadorned fingers. Fingers that had until just a short time ago been bathed in blood. In that moment I realized something important. Perhaps I'd known it all along, but her actions today confirmed it. She had the hands of a healer, not a killer.

"You aren't a murderer."

She frowned, a deep V forming in her brow. "What does that have to do with jewels?" she asked.

I looked down at the green gems in my palm. "Nothing." I met her eyes. "Your crime. You said you'd committed murder."

She didn't respond, for I hadn't asked her a question.

"That's not true, is it? The match, I know the match is true. Our connection—" I pointed between the two of us, "—is not a lie."

Tears filled her eyes. "No. We are not a lie."

"And the rest?" I asked, my voice soft. I felt as if the weight of Trion was in her response.

"Lies," she whispered, a tear slipping down her cheek. She wiped it away with the back of her hand.

I sighed, imminently pleased.

"Tell me. Tell me everything."

I sat on the rug before her as she told me what happened.

"I work in a hospital, a med unit, on Earth. People come there if they are sick or injured, like the wounded today. I save lives. That's my job. One night someone came in who'd been shot." She described to me what that meant, the kind of weaponry used. "He'd been stabilized and ready for a room. On Earth, it takes days or weeks to heal. While he was waiting, someone came into the hospital and killed him. He was part of a crime family—a family that does bad things—and his death was required to settle some kind of turf war between the families. That part of the story isn't important, only that I was the only witness, I saw the killer through the curtain that separated his bed from others."

I clenched the gems tightly in my grip. The idea of Eva

being that close to a killer—a real killer—had me ready to transport to Earth and hunt the man down.

"He didn't see me, didn't know I was there. When the police came, we were all questioned and I was able to identify the man. Turns out he's wanted for many such crimes, but has never been able to be convicted for them. He's a known assassin, with many deaths to pay for. And I am the only one who can stop him. My testimony would put him away, would bring down a very powerful and well-connected crime family."

Dread filled my gut at where this story was going. I knew what she would say next.

"They sent you away to keep you safe, so the killer couldn't reach you."

They'd sent her all the way to Trion.

She nodded. "Yet the only way I could do so was to join the Interstellar Bride Program as a criminal. On Earth, the worst criminals are expedited and my match was made quickly."

I was angry. Furious even. Eva had been forced to give up her life, to go off-planet, because she'd witnessed a crime. "You're the innocent one and instead of that *fark*, you were made out to be the criminal, the murderer. What Bertok and the others said to you."

I swallowed down the bitter anger in my throat.

"Yes, but I was matched to you," she replied.

I looked at her fiercely. She was right. We'd been matched because of this random act. It never would have happened otherwise. She would *never* be a criminal and therefore never would have been put in the Interstellar Bride Program. Had it been fate? It seemed like destiny to me.

"Then it doesn't matter. None of it. You're here, safe and away from the danger to you on Earth."

She came up onto her knees to move closer to me. Her pale eyes were bleak instead of relieved.

"I have to go back."

I stood abruptly. Her words hit me like a blow to the solar plexus. "What?"

She couldn't just leave. She'd just arrived. I'd just found her. She was mine and I was not giving her back.

"I have to testify. I have a personal transport nodule implanted in my skull." Her hand lifted to a spot behind her ear. "When it's time, it will transport me back to testify. Usually, all the matches for Earth's brides are permanent, but that's not true for me. They plan to bring me back to Earth for the trial. I have to go back."

"When? Why did you not tell me?"

"I don't know when. They said the trial would be in a couple of months. I was supposed to blend in here on Trion and hide until they summoned me."

"No. I won't give you up. Just have Doctor Rahm take the nodule out."

She shook her head slowly. "It doesn't work that way. It was part of the agreement. They wanted to keep me alive to testify. Obviously, I wanted to stay alive, so I agreed. I didn't know where they would send me or to whom. I knew nothing, just like you. I made them agree to bring me back, not only to testify and put the man in prison, but because I needed a way to go home."

My heart was beating so hard I was sure Eva could hear it. I felt it aching at the very idea of her being so many light-years away. I hadn't even liked her being in the harem across the outpost.

"And now? Do you want to go home?"

"I... I don't know."

Her indecision was fine with me. She didn't say yes. She didn't jump eagerly to her feet in anticipation of returning to Earth. She looked lost and confused. If she wanted to stay, then she was giving up her world, her way of life, forever. As a convict, she'd had no choice, but Eva had known all along that she could return home. She was conflicted about it.

It was my job to sway her, to make her stay. Perhaps she

read my thoughts, for she said, "I have to go. I don't have a choice. The transport technology will take me back. I don't even know when it's going to happen."

There had to be a way. I had to discover how to keep her. For now, I had to show her, to make her doubts go away. She had to know that she was mine. I'd said it over and over, had pushed her, bullied her even, into the idea. Now it was time to show her my real feelings, to convince her to stay through the connection we shared.

I moved back to the bed, tilted her chin up with my fingers so her eyes met mine. Held. "Is Eva really your name?"

"Yes."

"It doesn't matter that the bride program matched us. All that matters is what we think. I know you are my perfect match. I *feel* it."

Tears dripped down her cheeks. I knelt before her and opened my palm.

"The chain between your breasts marked you as mine for all to see, but it was a symbol of my power over you. You witnessed it firsthand in the meeting earlier. While I proved my possessiveness to the councilors, it was at a cost to you."

I affixed one of the green gems to the ring on her right nipple, then the other to the left.

"Now you are again marked as mine. These, however, I hope—" I lifted my gaze from her nipples to her eyes, "—you will wear because you are proud to be mine. They show that I am very much yours in return."

She was even lovelier without the chain. The gems made her pale skin glow and made her hair shine like fire. My cock throbbed in my pants, reminding me that while my heart might want to tell her of my feelings, my cock wanted to *show* her.

"It's too much," she replied.

I frowned and cupped both her breasts. "They are too much? They hurt?" Her skin was like the finest of silk, my palms so rough and dark against her tender flesh.

She shook her head. "The gems. They appear precious."

My worry eased. "*You* are precious." I grinned then, ready to shift from this mood. I did not share my feelings with others often—if ever—and I was ready to turn my time with Eva toward more carnal directions.

"Did the rings you wore do this?" I waved my hand in front of the gems and they began to vibrate. The piece that attached the gem to the ring was a stimulator that I could control.

"Oh," she gasped. "You have... you have many different kinds of toys."

"Toys? As in children?"

Her eyes fell closed and she thrust out her breasts. "No, toys for... for sex. Like the stimspheres."

I stroked the underside of one breast and she glanced at me. "Hmm, you liked those too much, I believe, especially if you consider them a toy. You like toys for sex?" While we were surely matched, I had much to learn.

"I have never used them in the past with another person, but so far, I think so."

I liked how she worded that sentence. It led me to believe the woman was much more adventurous in her desires than even she realized. Perhaps she'd just never had the opportunity to test her limits, which I would definitely provide to her now. "Eva, you *are* a bad girl." I grinned. Leaning on one elbow, I reached over the side of the bed to the small chest again. I tossed a variety of toys for sex onto the bed.

"Here, you have permission to play with these while I am in the bathing tube, but you may not come. Your pleasure belongs to me." Picking up one of the toys of sex, I handed it to her, then went to bathe.

My cock didn't care if I was clean or not, but I wanted to give her a few minutes to play with the items on her own before I used all of them, every single one of them, on her.

• • • • • • •

"Haven't found one you like?" Tark asked, stepping from the bathing unit. I looked up from the selection of space sex toys and my mouth went dry. I had yet to see Tark fully naked. Standing before me was a warrior. He was lethal-looking, so dark and brooding and with his size and formidable muscles, no one was a match for him. No wonder I submitted to him so easily. He just radiated power and judging by the way my pussy began to swell and soften for him, he was dripping in pheromones.

"Oh, I... um."

He grinned at my loss for words. Tilting his chin, he indicated what I held forgotten in my hand. "Do you want me to tell you what those are, or show you?"

I glanced down at the odd contraptions. One looked like a dildo but was shaped like tiered orbs, narrow at the top and wider at the bottom where my hand gripped it. The other was shaped like a U and was made of a smooth metal, I had no idea how it worked or where it went. I couldn't make it vibrate or anything.

I licked my lips. "Show me."

Coming over to the bed, he crawled up beside me and took it from me. Glancing down, he flicked at one of the gems on my nipples. "Like these?"

"Mmm," I murmured. The weight of the gems was much less than the chain and I felt almost naked without it. But the chain hadn't vibrated, hadn't done anything at all except exert a constant tug. The gems made my nipples tighten into hardened tips almost instantly after Tark had begun the vibrations. Cupping my breasts, even pressing on the nipples with my palms, didn't dull the ache the gems created. I wasn't sure how long I could last with such a simple torture. Now the man wanted to use some weird toys on me. I wasn't sure if I would survive. But I wanted to try.

"On your belly."

When I questioned him with a widening of my eyes, he

said, "Remember, *gara*, I will treat you as an equal outside of these walls—as long as your safety is not in jeopardy—but when it comes to fucking, you will submit to me. Always."

His voice was gentle, however, I heard the command there. He had stood aside and did as I ordered as I'd treated Mara, stepping back and allowing me to do my job until all of the patients were treated. I'd been in charge and he'd accepted that. But here, in this tent, he was the dominant one. I allowed it not only because it was true, but because I wanted it that way. I wanted Tark to tell me what to do, to take control, to tie me up and have his way. I even wanted him to spank me. This aroused me, pleased me. It filled a need inside me I didn't know I had. The bride program's testing had glimpsed into the deepest places within me, the places I'd hidden even from myself. Therefore, I didn't question him. Instead, I rolled over, careful of the gems on the blankets.

"Come up on your elbows if you need to. In fact, I'd like it if you did, for I enjoy seeing you adorned so prettily."

With my weight on my forearms, my back was arched and my breasts thrust out. Yes, based on the way his eyes darkened and his lids narrowed, he did like it. I felt... beautiful.

His hand drifted down my back, running over the ridges of my spine until he cupped one bottom cheek.

"So perfect."

"You're not going to spank me, are you?" I asked, tensing and waiting for that first resounding strike of his palm. I felt my pussy weep at the idea.

His eyes lifted from watching his hand to my face. "Do you want me to?"

I shook my head, although there was a little bit of untruth to it.

He held up the orbed toy. "This, this will fill your ass, stretch you open to take my cock."

My eyes widened, seeing the toy in a completely new way.

Grinning, he placed it on the bed and held up the U. "This one then." He placed it between the two dimples at my lower back. "During the first fucking, I touched you here." He'd slid his fingers down between the seam in my bottom and over my back entrance. "No, *gara*, don't tense up. Relax."

His hand moved away as he reached for something from the pile of toys he'd left on the bed. It was a vial of some kind and when he shifted his position so he could use both his hands, I began to worry. I had an idea of what he was going to do, what it was for, so I was apprehensive and slightly aroused by it at the same time. As he tipped the vial upside down, a drop of clear liquid came from the tip and dripped onto his fingers. The scent of it was familiar. Almonds.

I knew where the toys would go and I tried to relax. I watched over my shoulder as he used one hand to part the cheeks of my bottom and felt the slippery fluid coat me *there*.

As he gently circled me, very lightly, very slowly, he murmured to me. "Shh, good girl, breathe. Yes, relax. You came when my finger was inside you. Imagine what it will feel like when my cock is buried deep. This is much smaller than that other toy. Different. Trust me."

I did trust him, but I couldn't help but clench down at the idea of his cock filling me... there. He laughed at me, but I was not bothered. Well, not by that. I was getting very *bothered* by his attentions.

He picked up the vial and placed it directly against my virgin opening, easily letting the tip of it settle inside me. It was very small, so even as I clenched it was able to gain entrance. I felt warmth seep inside me. The sweet scent of it was strong, strong enough to bring back the dream from the processing center. God, I'd dreamt the smell of anal lubricant?

"This will make you slick, *gara*, I will never hurt you. That's it. Feel that? Yes, it's warm and it will ease the way of my finger, or the toy, and especially my cock."

I didn't know how much of the liquid he'd put inside of me, but I felt it going in quite far, the heat of it a surprise. It didn't hurt at all, but now I knew the depth at which he intended to fill me. Hopefully he'd prepare me using more than just adding lubrication.

Perhaps part of the match included mind-reading, for he said, "No cock today, *gara*. You're not ready... yet. Soon though. Soon you'll have me everywhere. I'll claim every part of you."

I gasped at the idea and the eager tone of his words. He lifted the toy off my lower back and parted me once again. This time, instead of his finger, I felt the cool metal press against me. He circled it and pressed in at the same time as he continued to whisper to me. Words of praise, words of desire and it relaxed me, made the object slide into my ass, stretching me open in the process.

Once it had breached me there, Tark wasn't done, for now I knew why there was a U to it. The other end of it slid easily and without any coaxing into my pussy. Further and further it went in until I was filled front and back with hard metal. It wasn't as thick as Tark, so as my body clenched down on the foreign object, I knew right away it wasn't enough.

Tark stroked his hand over my bottom. "How does that feel?"

I glanced at him, the warrior had changed into a lover. His cock stood thick and proud from his body and I knew he wished he was fully seated in me instead of the toy.

"It's... deep. But not as big as you."

He grinned wickedly. "Flattery, *gara*. I like it. But can my cock do this?"

All at once the metal began to vibrate.

"Shit!" I cried, my arms collapsing and I fell onto the bed. "Does... does everything on Trion vibrate?" I asked, gasping.

I couldn't lie still. I had to move, for the U toy was hitting every sensitive spot inside me, some that I never even knew I had. Feeling something deep in my ass should have felt bad, but it felt like heaven. This, this was like my dream. The intense pleasure, the scent of almonds. Oh, my God, I was going to come. I stuck my butt up in the air, wiggled it, fell to my side and grabbed my breasts, trying to ease the ache in them.

"Tark!" I cried.

He avidly watched me writhe on the bed, clearly pleased with himself.

"Master," he said, his voice a deep growl.

He flipped me onto my back, spread my legs, and settled between them. He wasn't gentle, but I didn't need gentle. The feelings were incredible and I was dying a blissful death. Sweat broke out on my skin and my heart was pounding. I could barely catch my breath let alone cry out.

My eyes had fallen shut and I was lost in the pleasure. That was why I hadn't known he'd put his head between my thighs until I felt his mouth latch onto my clit. I lifted my head and looked at him down the length of my body. He was looking at me, his mouth glistening and slick with my juices.

"Master," I cried.

"You need to come, Eva?"

He flicked his tongue over my clit, his warm breath fanning the sensitive bud. With his hands, he gripped my hips, stopped my wriggling.

"Yes."

"Say it."

"I want to come... master."

"Good girl. You may come now."

He put his mouth on me and sucked, his tongue flicking out as he somehow tugged on me. I had no idea what he was doing and I didn't care. He was as skilled with his mouth as his fingers and his cock.

I came with a scream. It was so hard that my thighs clenched Tark's head. Surely I would crack his skull like a tree nut, but I didn't care. The vibrations in my ass were so incredible that tears rolled down my cheeks. I couldn't take it. It was too much. Between my ass, my pussy, and Tark's ruthless assault on my clit, I came again. Then again.

"Stop. Stop!" I cried. I was going to die of pleasure.

All at once, the vibrations in the U toy and the nipple gems tapered off, then stopped completely. Tark continued to lick at my clit, but gently, as if easing me down.

"Is that all your body can give me, *gara?*"

"Yes." I couldn't breathe, couldn't think. I was out of my mind, my body was not my own, it was his.

"Yes, what?" He nipped at my clit with his teeth, gently, and I moaned, my body a writhing mass of highly stimulated nerves.

"Master. Yes, master." He was the master of my body, and now, I was afraid, master of my heart as well. I trusted him. He made me feel safe and cared for, protected and adored. With him, I didn't have to hide my desire or my fire, in his arms I could let everything go. I could fall, and he would catch me.

"Who owns your pleasure, Eva?"

Was this a trick question? He pulled the toy inside me halfway out, then slowly pushed it back inside. My hips lifted toward his mouth of their own volition. My body was like a finely tuned instrument, and he was playing me. "You do, master."

"Yes, I do." He smiled, right before he turned the vibrations back on. "And I will tell you when you've had enough." Tark wiggled the toy and attacked my clit with his mouth, suckling and fucking me with the toy until I arced up off the bed like a bowstring, unable to resist his carnal dominance over my body as he forced me to another peak. Unable to cry out, I whimpered when my release came with the fury of a tornado ripping through my body.

Before I could catch my breath, he pulled the toy from my well-used body and tossed it aside. Coming up on his knees, Tark knelt between my splayed thighs. He gripped one of my hands, lifted it above my head, then the other, holding them tightly in place as he secured them with a thick leather tie. I tugged at the hold and knew he would not free me. He would take me as he wanted. My pussy clenched around empty air, the pain of my arousal caused the lips of my pussy to pulse with pain in time to my heart's rapid beat. I needed him inside me, filling me. Making me his. I needed his pleasure, his possession. I needed to be what he wanted, to give him what he wanted.

"It's time to fuck you now."

I nodded my head even as silent tears streamed from the corners of my eyes. The intensity of his possession, of his control over my body, of my release, overwhelmed me and I couldn't hold back the tears. Those tears were me, my soul, the emotional dam bursting open inside me here, now, in the safety of his embrace.

I was his, body and soul, and would deny him nothing. While the toy had been amazing, it hadn't been Tark's cock and I craved his hard length stretching me wide. I needed the connection. I needed to see him strain, to watch him lose himself in the pleasure only my body could give him. I needed to know that he was mine.

He lined himself up and slid into me in one smooth, long stroke. He dropped down onto his forearms so his head was right above mine and filled me completely. I was pinned down, my hands secure above my head, my hips pressed into the soft bed by his. I couldn't move. I couldn't do anything but let him fuck me.

Holding himself still, he murmured, "*Gara.*"

Lowering his head, he kissed me as he moved. Fucking and kissing. He was remarkably gentle and this… this was something more. This was a validation that we belonged to each other. He'd most certainly given me my pleasure, but I knew—I could *feel*—that I was more to him than just a woman to fuck and breed. He'd changed, even in the ridiculously short time I'd been on Trion. His hardness, the angles and planes of frustration and power, were softened. I'd done that to him.

I could ease his worry, soften the burden that was on his shoulders as high councilor. In this moment, he was able to lose himself in me, seek pleasure and comfort. Not as high councilor, not as the leader of his people, not as powerful man who had many people looking to him for guidance.

With me, he was simply Tark, the man. His motions shifted from a gentle glide and the sweet friction of his cock returned me to the brink of release as if my desire was a tinder rekindled to bright fire. Swiftly, his pace quickened as if he were reaching for something. I understood.

"Tark. Let go." I used his name on purpose, let him know that he didn't even have to worry about protecting me in this moment. He could just succumb to the pleasure he found in my body, in the release that I could give to him.

He tilted his head up and looked at me. Sweat dripped onto my breast.

"I can't lose control. I never lose control." He ran his hands along my arms and squeezed my wrists. "I don't want to hurt you," he replied, his hips shifting and churning.

Bringing my legs up, I pressed my knees into his sides so he could fill me even deeper.

I shook my head. "You won't. You *can't*."

Perhaps it was my tone, or the look on my face, or the way my inner walls clenched on his cock, but the mask slipped. His face hardened, his jaw clenched tight, and his eyes closed. Hooking the back of my knee in the crook of his elbow, he angled me up and drove into me. I cried out because he'd filled me almost too full, but he didn't stop.

"Yes," I cried, letting him know I wanted it. I did. I wanted all of him. If we were so well matched, I could take it. I could handle whatever he gave me, I *needed* to accept him, all of him. I needed to please him, to make him happy, to submit to his desire. I met him each time he thrust into me; his grip tightened on my leg and my hip and I knew my wild response was pushing him to the edge of his control. The sound of fucking filled the tent—rough, carnal, and wet.

"I want a baby, Tark. Your baby. Give it to me," I panted. I did. I wanted to give him the baby he desired, the one I'd longed for but never imagined. I'd been appalled by the idea of being bred, that Tark's main goal for a mate was to find a woman that was fertile and could give him the heir he needed.

But this wasn't what we were doing. We weren't fucking over a ceremonial stand. We weren't being watched or recorded for the bride program processing center. We were just a man and a woman who needed each other and showed our desires, our reason for being by coming together in such a way. I was powerful. I could turn Tark into a rutting animal, eager and desperate for his release, until everything but filling me was cleared from his mind.

"Please, Tark."

"You want it, *gara*?" he growled.

"Yes!"

"You want me? Only me? You'll stay with me and be my mate?"

I opened my eyes and he was gazing at me. My nipples brushed against his chest the way I was arched up, my hands above my head.

I'd barely seen anything of Trion. I only knew that Outpost Nine was primitive and in the middle of the desert. Was the rest of Trion this way? Were all the people like Bertok or Mara? I longed to find out, as long as Tark was with me, by my side.

What did Earth have waiting for me? There was no match. No Tark. The decision was simple.

"Yes."

Reaching between us, Tark stroked his thumb over my clit, once, twice, and I came.

I arched my back even more and cried out, feeling Tark stiffen above me, filling me full and shouting his own release. Thick seed shot into me, filling me to overflowing. Greedily, my body clenched and milked Tark's cock, pulling it in deep.

"Yes," I said.

"*Fark*, yes," Tark replied, trying to catch his breath. He lowered his upper body to the side, so his heavy weight was not upon me, but kept his cock buried deep. The endorphins from all the fucking had me feeling euphoric and replete. Feeling Tark above me I felt safe and cherished and very well claimed. He released the tie holding my wrists, stroked a hand over my cheek, wiping away the silent tears that continued to fall.

"I know, *gara*. I know. You are safe with me." He cradled me then, and as wild as our fucking had been, he was now a gentle giant holding me safe in the storm of my own emotions. I couldn't hold anything back, not my desire, my pleasure, or the deepest, darkest corners of my heart and soul. And there, in his arms, I didn't fight my emotions, because I didn't have to. The mask society forced me to wear was gone. He'd stripped me bare and held me protected and secure in his arms.

"Promise me, Tark. Never leave me," I said to him.

"*Gara*, you're the one who's leaving. I will contact our liaison at the program, see if something can be arranged so that I may accompany you to Earth, and bring you safely home."

I stiffened beneath him. "Really? You can do that?"

"I will do whatever must be done to keep you safe. You are mine. I understand that you must do what is honorable and right. You must return to offer your testimony, but I will not allow you to face a brutal killer alone."

I snuggled into his chest with a happy sigh. How I'd gotten so lucky, I had no idea. But Tark was indeed the only man I could imagine spending the rest of my life with. He was my perfect match.

A slight buzz sounded in the room and I shook my head to clear it as a strange voice spoke into the silence.

"*The transport protocol for Eve Daily had been activated.*"

The personal transport nodule hummed against my ear and I could hear the voice clearly in my head. Had Tark heard it, too?

Tark slipped his cock from my body and yanked me up onto my knees. "What was that?" he said, all softness and pleasure from our fucking gone. His seed dripped down my thighs as I knelt on the bedding.

"I... I think it was the transport nodule and I'm being returned to Earth."

My heart started to pound and Tark's hands gripped my upper arms.

"Now? You can't go. We just agreed you'd stay." He looked frantic, as if this was the one thing completely out of his control and there was nothing he could do, no matter how much he fought or talked his way out of it.

"I want to stay with you," I said, wrapping my arms around him and hugging him tightly.

"We can take the transporter from you, cut it out of your body."

I shook my head against his chest, the springy hairs there soft and ticklish on my cheek. "I must put the man away. It is the honorable thing to do."

"I know of honor, *gara*, but it is dangerous. You do not have to confront this killer on your own. We will contact the authorities on Earth and arrange for me to accompany you."

"I don't think there's time. I should be safe. I'll be protected by the police and the prosecutors. They will offer me their protection," I countered.

He pushed me away from him so he could look me in the eyes. "And yet they had no faith in their ability to keep you safe before. That is why they sent you here, to me."

"*Thirty seconds to transport.*"

"Tark, it's happening now. I'm sorry," I pleaded, hoping he'd understand that I had to go. I had to make things right on my world.

"You've done nothing wrong," he sighed, but I felt the fierceness in his hold. "Know this, Eva. There is no one in this galaxy for me but you. You know this."

I nodded as tears dripped down my cheeks.

"*Five.*"

"I will miss you," I told him.

"*Four.*"

"Eva!" His eyes widened.

"*Three.*"

"There's no one on Earth for me," I vowed, lifting up onto my knees to kiss him.

"*Two.*"

He pulled back, his breath mingling with mine. He curled his hand around my nape, kept me close. "You are my mate, my heart."

"*One.*"

"Master," I said as I no longer felt his touch, could not detect his spicy scent, could no longer see him.

CHAPTER NINE

I didn't wake gradually from the transport as I had the first time. I woke up with a start as if I had a bad dream, jolting upright with a gasp.

"Good, she's awake," someone said. It wasn't Tark.

I blinked my eyes and looked around.

I was in a small room with a wooden desk and chairs. Two men sat across from me, studying me closely.

"Robert," I said, perhaps more to myself because I recognized him than because I was glad to see him. The district attorney wore his usual crisp suit and was eyeing me carefully, perhaps wondering if the transport would have returned me misshapen or missing a limb or perhaps even naked.

I gasped and looked down at myself. I couldn't help the sigh that escaped when I saw I wore a plain white blouse and skirt. I felt the usual heeled shoes on my feet, but couldn't see what kind or color because they were hidden beneath the table. Patting my hair, I discovered the wild mess had been pulled up into a neat style and pinned in place at the back of my head.

"Do you feel all right?" Robert asked. I glanced at him and the man beside him.

"Sorry, Eva, this is Special Agent Davidson with the FBI. He arranged for your transport off-planet."

I nodded to both men. "Robert, I... it hasn't been three months yet. What happened?" It had only been a few days since I was sent to Trion; surely the trial hadn't been moved up so far.

Both men frowned. "What are you talking about? Eva, it's been four months."

"Are you sure you're all right, ma'am?"

I was confused, my mind a blur. I'd only been on Trion, one, two, three, yes, three days. How could four months have passed? "I think... I think time is different on Trion."

"You went to Trion?" Robert's eyes lit up, eager like a child.

I nodded.

"Well, what was it like? Is it true the matching program works?"

I thought of Tark and how, just moments ago—at least to me—I was in his arms. I hugged myself as if I could feel him still, but no. It wasn't the same. I recognized the temperature control of the rooms in buildings on Earth. On Trion, the air, while hot, was not overly so. It was... balmy.

My arms pressed against my nipples and I felt the rings and the gems Tark had put there. They were still there!

"Are you sure you're all right?" the FBI agent asked.

"I just transported from Trion, so please give me a minute to adjust. I would assume that I am the only person to return since the program is traditionally one-way."

"It is," the man confirmed. "We programmed your transport so that you would arrive in the courthouse—as you can tell from the room we're in—and dressed appropriately for the hearing."

That explained the rings and the gems. The man didn't know what the Trion customs were, what Tark had done to me, therefore he didn't know they needed to be removed on transport back. He assumed I just needed to be put into the correct clothes for the trial, nothing more.

I was relieved actually, for the nipple rings, the gems, were all that I had left of Tark. I was on the opposite side of the galaxy from him and there was nothing I could do about it.

"I'm fine. If I could have a glass of water, then we can go over whatever you need me to say. Then I'd like to go home."

I was going to cry, but I swallowed back the tears. I couldn't cry now, in front of these men. I couldn't let them know that I'd fallen for my match, that I wanted to stay on Trion. It didn't matter now. I was going to do the right thing, put the man behind bars, and then I would return to work and get on with my life.

• • • • • • •

A week later, the trial was over. The man had been found guilty and sent to prison. His sentencing would occur in the next few months, but my part was done. Since I wasn't actually Evelyn Day, my personal record never showed the fake conviction and my sentencing to the bride program. Instead of returning to my life as I'd suspected—and I'd been told would happen before I left for Trion—I'd been put into the witness protection program. The threat to my life had not gone away when the trial was over. The man had put a price on my head and I was not safe.

The FBI agent dumped me in a small town in Iowa with a new name, unable to practice medicine. I was given a job as a school librarian. I missed Tark keenly, night and day. I lay in bed at night—in a strange new home—and played with the gems on my nipple rings. No matter what I did, I couldn't get them to vibrate. I refused to remove them, for they were a part of me. I only had to wear padded bras and be cautious in my shirt selection, otherwise no one knew. I had no intention of sharing them, for what could I say?

They were mine. Mine and Tark's, and they were private. My pussy was still bare. I'd originally thought I'd been shaved, but after the few days on Trion and the time back on Earth, none of the hair between my legs had grown back. I touched myself there and just like with the stimspheres, no matter how I played with my clit, I could not climax. I needed Tark.

All of the men on Earth seemed so small, so weak in comparison. I found I used Tark as a basis for the *perfect* man and not one person I knew, or met, or came across in the grocery store matched up.

I had no friends in my new life. I had no family, since both of my parents had died when I was young. I was alone and sad and I felt as if a piece of me was missing. I was the same person I'd been before I witnessed the murder, but stepping back—or off-planet—made me see what my life here had been like. And that barren existence was a far cry from what I wanted it to be. Before Tark, work had been my life. When I'd left Earth, I barely had real friends, no family.

I wanted Tark. I needed him so intensely that I was willing to give up Earth for him. I touched myself, circling my fingers over my clit, heating my body as I thought of my mate, wishing it was his hand and his mouth on me. As he'd said, my pleasure belonged to him, so as I felt arousal, I cried out in desperation for his touch. Then I cried my heart out.

Something had to be done. I had to get back to Tark and I knew just the person to talk to.

· · · · · · ·

"Enter."

At my shout, the flap opened and Mara and Davish were escorted into my tent. Mara looked returned to health. Her cheeks were full of color, her hair a long mane down her back. Her shift dress was free of blood and the modest robe she wore over it shielded most of her body from my gaze.

Not that it was needed. Nothing about the woman appealed to me. She was attractive enough and she was

Davish's mate, but I didn't like her lithe build, her small breasts, the usual dour expression. I wanted Eva.

It had only been a day since she had literally slipped through my fingers, transported back to Earth. I felt empty and hollow, as if a part of me had been yanked and taken with her across the vast expanse of space that separated us.

"High councilor, we came to bid your mate many thanks." Davish looked about the room for her. If he'd taken Mara from the harem, he knew Eva was not there.

"You are both well?" I asked.

"Yes, high councilor," Mara whispered as Davish nodded.

"Good. While your visit is appreciated, my mate is not here."

They both frowned in confusion.

"She was transported back to Earth."

Mara looked shocked. "Was it because of me? I was... unkind to her." She looked embarrassed about it, ashamed even. "I made her angry, which upset you. Your denial of her is my fault."

She lowered herself to her knees and dipped her head.

I looked to Davish, who clenched his jaw at the news, which was obviously a surprise to him. I was not happy to learn that Mara had been hurtful to Eva, but it was not my place to punish her.

"Rise," I said. She did, but kept her head down. "She was not transported at my wishes. Quite the contrary. Her testimony was needed to send a man to prison."

"She was not a murderer?" Davish asked.

I shook my head.

Something akin to admiration lit his eyes. "Your mate is honorable," Davish remarked. "Her actions yesterday were one example. Leaving a mate because of duty is another. I will tell the council."

Mara squeezed her hands together. "She saved my life and I will be forever grateful."

The couple left without more comment, the tent empty

once again. I saw the ceremonial stand in the corner, the bed with the blankets that still held Eva's scent. I dropped my head into my hands and relived the conversation I'd had a few hours ago. I had successfully contacted the Interstellar Bride Program liaison for Trion and was coldly informed that if my mate had chosen to leave me, there was nothing they could do. It was my fault for not enticing her, for not pleasing her. My name would be placed back on the register of available males from Trion, at the bottom of the list, since I could not satisfy a female.

I wanted to leap through the communication screen and strangle the female officer with my bare hands. She implied that I was not worthy. That Eva left me because I was not good enough to deserve her.

Perhaps that bitch was correct. Eva was gone. If I'd been a better mate, I would have questioned Eva earlier, I would have had time to prevent the transport from taking her back without me. If I'd acted on my instincts, the instincts that insisted she was not a murderer, I could have forced the truth from her lips and made arrangements to protect her on her trip to Earth and keep her at my side.

I'd failed as her mate, but her brief presence in my life haunted me. Memories of her taunted me everywhere I looked, but she was gone. Forever.

I tossed a bowl filled with fruit against the wall, but it did nothing to make me feel better.

CHAPTER TEN

I was once again in the small room at the processing center, although this time I wasn't wearing the prison garb and I wasn't strapped in. Warden Egara stood next to my processing chair and glared at the FBI agent who sat in a small plastic chair in the corner of the room. Today her suit was navy blue, the insignia on her chest was still red, almost as red as her cheeks. Warden Egara was clearly furious with Agent Davidson.

"Is this DNA scan correct?" She raised her eyebrows and scowled at the FBI agent. "This woman's DNA sample is already on file in our system. She is not supposed to be on Earth. According to our records, she is, at this very moment, on Trion, with her mate. And her name is not Eva Daily, it's Evelyn Day."

"Yes, the DNA is correct. But her real name is Eva Daily." He had the good sense to sound contrite.

"And how did this woman return to Earth without permission from the Interstellar Bride Program?" She crossed her arms and I would swear she grew two inches taller as she towered over the seated man. When Agent Davidson didn't respond, she put her hands on her hips.

"Are you aware, Agent Davidson, that in deceiving me,

as an official representative of the interstellar coalition, and as head of this Interstellar Bride Program processing center, I could bring charges against you with the interstellar council? Fraud and impersonation are crimes on all worlds, agent." Warden Egara looked ready to take his sidearm from him and shoot him dead on the spot. I jumped off the table to stand between them.

"Please, warden. The matching process was perfect. I'm sorry I lied to you. I didn't have a choice. But now, I just want to go home." I hoped the longing and sincerity of my request would convince her to help me. This strange, formidable woman literally held my future in her hands. She was the only one who had the power to send me back to the man I loved. "Please. Help me. I just want to go back to him."

"You are aware that *this time*, Miss Day, or Daily, or whatever name you are using this week," Warden Egara gave the FBI agent a withering glance, "you will not be able to return to Earth."

"Yes. I know. I don't want to be here. I want to be on Trion, with my matched mate."

Warden Egara's eyes softened just a bit, and I caught a glimpse of the beauty she'd be if she ever smiled. "The matching process is truly miraculous, Eva. I have witnessed it many times. It's why I protect my brides so fiercely. The warriors who protect us, who protect all life on coalition worlds, deserve to be loved. They deserve to find true happiness. And when someone fucks with my warriors, I am *not* amused." This last she directed at Agent Davidson, who had the grace to blush.

"My apologies. I already told you, I swear, I'll never use your program to hide a bride again. You have my word." The FBI agent held his hands up in complete surrender. I'd called Agent Davidson two weeks ago and told him I wanted to go back to Trion. At first, he hadn't understood why I would want to do that. I wasn't a prisoner and I'd certainly given more of myself than any other witness he'd ever helped before. He didn't understand the matching process and most likely never would. Even though I'd tried to explain the connection I felt to Tark, more than once, he'd forced me to wait two full weeks, *to think about it*, before he would fulfill my request.

They had been two very long weeks of waiting. Knowing he would help me get back to Trion, and to Tark, filled me with eager anticipation. This time, I knew where I was going. This time, I knew who I was going to be with. This time, I *wanted* to go. If Tark wanted to bend me over a ceremonial stand and fuck me for the entire council to see, I didn't even mind. Well, maybe a little, but it would be a worthy price to pay to be back in his arms and his life.

"Please, Warden Egara. Send me home." I whispered the words as butterflies danced in my stomach. I sat back down on the chair and waited impatiently for the woman to start the process.

"We do not need to complete the matching tests again as they have been done once. However, protocol demands I ask, do you wish to reject your match and be sent to a different warrior?"

I couldn't help but smile. "I choose to keep my match to High Councilor Tark of Trion, permanently."

Agent Davidson angled his head and studied me. "You love him." It wasn't a question and he said it with a hint of awe.

Nodding, I replied, "I do. I can, for a fact, Warden Egara, say that your matching program is indeed very good."

The woman puffed up with pride and I could see she was eager to ask me questions about my time on another world, but her job took precedence. "That is good to hear." She looked down at the screen she held and swiped at it a few times. "You are ready to transport to Trion and are permanently matched to High Councilor Tark. There will be no changes allowed."

I grinned and gripped the armrests of the chair.

Anticipation unlike I'd ever known before coursed through my veins. *Come on, woman. Push the fucking button.* "No. There will be no changes allowed."

"Goodbye, Eva." Agent Davidson gave me a reassuring nod.

Warden Egara pushed the processing chair toward the wall, but this time I was excited to see the small room appear beside me. I welcomed the bite of the needle in my neck and the bright blue light that meant I was going back to Trion. I looked over and caught Warden Egara's eye. "Thank you."

She actually smiled. "Your transport will begin in three, two, one."

• • • • • • •

"This concludes the meeting of the council. We will meet again next year. During that time, safe travels and peace in your region."

I stood, the men before me did as well. Even though we'd spent a week together working through the agenda, councilors stood and chatted, milling about. All I wanted to do was get the *fark* out of Outpost Nine. It only held memories of Eva. I saw her everywhere I went. And, knowing that she was not a murderer but instead a healer, everyone stopped me to ask after her. I'd finally forced Goran to post a notice of Eva's return to Earth so I did not have to repeat it again and again.

Warning squawks came from the guards' communication units. Everyone froze in place, awaiting word of the danger.

"A transport, high councilor." The lead guard approached me, then looked down at his unit. "Unscheduled."

"Origin?" I asked. While the guards could defend against attackers on Trion, defending an outpost against transport attacks directly from other worlds was much more difficult.

"Earth."

The man looked up at me and I knew his thoughts.

"Eva," I murmured. "It has to be."

"No matching has been recorded from that planet. I believe you are right."

"How long?" I asked, already running to the lone transport pad on the outpost. It was close.

"Thirty seconds." The guard ran beside me, the rest following behind.

I'd make it in ten. "Switch your weapons to stun. If it turns out to be my mate, I don't want anyone to shoot her."

The guard nodded and I glanced at the others.

"Stand back," I boomed. "No one moves until we assess the transport."

Hope swelled in my chest as I stopped inside the tent and watched the empty spot before me. Slowly, a body materialized and it was, indeed, Eva. Sprawled on the dark black transport pad she appeared to be asleep, she looked... *fark*, she looked like the most amazing thing I'd ever seen.

The two guards who had entered behind me stood down and put their weapons away. I knelt beside her and scooped her up into my arms. She wore the slip dress and nothing else. With her pressed against my chest, I could feel the rings in her nipples and the gems I'd put there before she'd returned to Earth.

The soft feel of her, the scent of her skin, the silky feel of her hair, *fark*, it was hard to believe she was in my arms. I'd thought I'd never see her again and yet... how had she been able to return?

I carried her back to the main tent, eager to share the good news. I wasn't sure what to expect from those gathered, but instead of disdain or hostility on the faces of the councilors, they all looked pleased and perhaps even amazed at her return.

Stroking her hair back from her face, I talked to her, whispering in her ear and waiting for her to wake. It had taken hours the last time so I had to assume—

"Tark?" she murmured, shifting in my arms.

"Shh, *gara*, I've got you."

Her eyes opened at the sound of my voice and she stared at me, her body stiffening. "Tark!" she repeated as she wrapped her arms around me and gripped me tightly.

Even though I could hear whispers all around us, my focus was solely on my mate.

"You came back," I whispered into her ear.

She nodded against my chest.

"May I ensure she is well, high councilor?" Doctor Rahm asked, standing a respectable distance away.

"*Gara*, will you let the doctor ensure you are well after your transport?"

She stiffened. "Not another probe."

"No. No probes. I will hold you the entire time. You traveled across the galaxy not once for me, but twice."

"All right."

I gave a slight head nod and Doctor Rahm held up a sensor and moved it above her body. He didn't touch her, didn't even look at her, only at the display on the medical unit. His eyes widened, then did another pass, then turned it to face me. I read the display and my heart leapt into my throat. Pride filled me and my chest ached.

"*Gara*," I growled.

"Hmm," she murmured.

"You... you're—" The words caught in my throat.

"Yes."

I didn't want this moment when I discovered my mate was carrying my child to be shared by anyone. There was a roomful of councilors to contend with first, and then I would have her to myself. The meetings were over. We would leave Outpost Nine as soon as she was well enough to travel. Now that she was with child, I wanted her safe in the palace more than ever.

"I am well, Tark. Please, let me stand."

Carefully, I placed her on her feet, yet kept a possessive grip about her waist. She laid her head against my side and I forced myself to look away from her and at the others in the tent.

"Lady consort," Councilor Roark said, lowering to one knee before her. It was the traditional position of respect and honor when offering allegiance. All members of the council offered it to me at the death of my father and during my investiture.

"Lady consort," the other members repeated together, also lowering to one knee before her.

Eva glanced at them, then up at me. "They are giving you their respect."

"But—"

"We are glad of your return, lady consort."

Commotion at the entrance to the tent turned everyone's heads. Davish stepped inside with Mara. The woman ran to the stage and dropped to her knees as well.

"I am sorry, Eva—"

"Lady consort," Roark advised.

Mara licked her lips and looked contrite. "Lady consort, I am so very sorry for how I treated you. I owe you a debt for saving my life." Mara sounded remorseful, looked it even, however I knew her to be duplicitous.

"I treated you as I would any other person, here on Trion, or on Earth. I hope that your life debt is not the only reason you now offer your friendship. I hope that any friendship be willingly given. I do not know very many women here on Trion and I will need friends that I can trust."

Mara looked surprised by the words, but I understood. Eva needed those about her, the people who would care for her, to know who she really was. She did not want Mara to take a bended knee out of gratitude or debt. A small smile formed on Mara's mouth, for once it seemed given without malice. "Yes, my lady, I would like that."

"Then you must call me Eva."

"Enough," I said. "I assume, Councilor Bertok, that there is no need for another ceremonial fucking?" Since Eva was already carrying my child, the twisted old bastard would have to find his pleasure elsewhere.

The older man looked at the ground. "No, high councilor. There is no question she is the rightful lady consort."

I nodded. "Good. As Doctor Rahm has cleared her from her transport, my mate and I will bid you farewell. Safe journey to all as you return to your homelands."

Many of those gathered murmured replies, but I scooped Eva up into my arms and fled the group, practically running to my tent. Eva had returned, her belly filled with my child, and I wanted her all to myself. Forever.

• • • • • • •

"How did you return to me?" Tark asked as soon as he'd placed me on his bed. I grabbed his hand, pulling him down with me when he would have stepped back. I didn't want space. I wanted to revel in the feel of him, the scent of him. I wanted... everything.

I'd spent weeks longing for him as I waited for Agent Davidson to finalize my transport. As he sat beside me, I told Tark everything about my time on Earth.

I shivered as I talked about the trial and how I'd felt staring into the eyes of a killer. I told him how lonely I'd been without him, and how they'd tried to give me a hollow shell of a life in witness protection. I described the details of my lonely and very empty apartment. I'd told him about Warden Egara's seemingly endless list of questions as we'd waited for the DNA results to confirm my story.

I'd answered her honestly, especially when she'd asked me about my match with Tark. I wanted everyone to know that the bride program's matching program really did work. I'd even agreed to film a small advertisement for the program before I left. Warden Egara was desperate to get more brides from Earth, preferably more volunteers, not criminals. She felt very strongly that the warriors protecting Earth deserved true happiness and worthy females as mates.

Looking at my mate, I felt completely happy with everything I'd said in that recording session, and I hoped some lucky Earth girl would take a chance on love on another world.

"Did you know about the baby when you... left?" He looked at my body as if I were a fragile piece of glass, perhaps worried that he'd hurt me or the baby.

"No. Only when they assessed me for transport." I paused.

He tilted his head, then dropped to his knees before me.

"The first time, I let the matching program decide," I told him. "This time, I named you, High Councilor Tark of Trion, as my permanent match. No trial period. No processing. You aren't ever getting rid of me. This time, I claimed you, Tark. You're mine forever."

"Oh, Eva," he groaned and pulled me in for a kiss. It was rough and desperate and full of heat and love and I needed all of it so, so badly.

"I missed you," he murmured against my mouth. "*Fark*, it was like my heart was ripped out of my chest when you transported."

"Time is different on Earth. While I was only here a few short days, it had been four months on Earth. Tark, we were apart for weeks."

"It was just yesterday," he said, thinking. "That was long enough."

"It was torture."

"Oh, *gara*. You're here now and I swear I'll never let you go."

"About that ceremonial first fucking," I said, biting my lip.

He arched one of his dark brows and smirked.

"Yes?"

"I think since I've left and come back, another may be in order."

"You want me to call Goran in to witness? The council?"

I shook my head and came up onto my knees, grabbed

the hem of my slip dress, and lifted it over my head.

A sound similar to a growl erupted from Tark's chest. Instead of pouncing on me as I'd perhaps expected—I wanted to jump him—his hand came out and flicked over the gem on my left nipple.

"Your breasts are bigger. I would have learned the truth of your pregnancy just by looking at your body."

The idea that the man knew my breasts so well only validated our match even further. That direction of thought was quickly lost when he cupped them and continued to run his thumbs over my now tender tips.

"It didn't work," I said, pouting. When he frowned, I added, "The vibration."

"You mean this?" He waved his hand over my breasts and the gems began to vibrate.

"Oh, yes," I cried, thrusting my breasts into his palms.

He knelt on the bed and forced me to lie back, then came down on top of me. He kissed me, long and deep.

"I want to fuck you." He pressed his cock against my center. "What about the baby?"

"You think fucking me will hurt the baby?"

He looked so unsure of himself, so vulnerable. He was in charge in the bedroom, but in this moment, the baby was. He might be dominant and commanding, tying me down and spanking me, but he would never hurt me.

I could feel how much he wanted me, could see it in his eyes, hear it in his voice, feel it in his kiss, but he was willing to sacrifice for his child.

"As a doctor, I can assure you that fucking will not hurt an unborn child." I shifted and Tark let me up. I reached over the bed to look for his small trunk. It was exactly where it had been before I left. I found the toy I wanted and looked at him over my shoulder.

"Or you can use this." Was I being too forward? Would he be shocked by my boldness? I'd come across the galaxy for him. I wasn't going to hold anything back now. "Perhaps you might find taking me here less worrisome."

His narrowed gaze slid down my back and landed on my bottom.

"You want me to fuck your ass, *gara*?"

The idea had my nipples hardening impossibly more. I could feel my wetness between my legs and my thighs were slick with it.

"Maybe not now, but you can prepare me."

His eyes went impossibly black and his jaw clenched. I could see his cock pressing against the front of his pants. He stood beside the bed and stripped. "Get the oil," he commanded.

With eager fingers, I reached back into the chest and found a vial of the almond-scented oil. I poured a little onto my fingers and put the container beside the toy on the bed.

Swiping my fingers together, I warmed it and the scent I'd grown to love, to obsess about, drifted to my nose. Almonds. I coated one hard nipple, then the other, with the glistening liquid. Tark stopped and just stared at me, watched my fingers.

"I dreamed of this scent when I was gone," I said.

Tark grabbed my hips and flipped me over onto my back. He spread my thighs wide and settled between them. His breath fanned over my pussy. "I dreamed of this scent, this taste, while you were gone."

He lowered his head, put his mouth on me, and made me come. It didn't take long, for I was eager for a Tark-induced orgasm and he was voracious.

I lay sweaty and limp, my legs splayed wide and my fingers tangled in his dark hair. I had no shame, no modest bone left in my body. He came up over me to place a soft kiss on my still flat belly.

He angled his head. "Roll over, Eva."

I eagerly complied. Scooping a hand around my waist, he pulled me back and up so that my ass was high and right before him. Reaching for the vial of oil, he parted my cheeks and I felt the slow, warm glide as drop after drop of oil fell onto my back entrance. Using his thumb, he circled slowly and carefully, watching me.

"I won't go away this time," I said.

His thumb stopped, but didn't move. I wiggled beneath his palm urging him on. I reached up and touched behind my ear. There was now an indent in the bone of my skull, where the transport nodule had been before. "See, it's not there, Tark. It's gone. I'm not going back to Earth. Ever."

For a flicker in time, I saw anguish on his face, but when I pushed back against him again, it was replaced by a gaze so filled with heat I sucked in a breath.

His hand lifted, then struck my bottom. I jolted at the contact. "Tark!"

"I was so mad." He began to spank me in earnest, one side then the other. It wasn't the hardest spanking he'd given me, but it was pretty darn close. I remained on my forearms and held still, allowing him to unleash the pent-up frustration. I, too, needed this rough handling, needed the focus that the spanking gave me. I reveled in his attention, felt each stinging swat and thought only on the next one. It was a short-lived spanking and when he was done, he cupped my bottom with both hands, stroking the warm skin. I felt my pussy dripping with need.

Glancing over my shoulder at him, I said, "You punished me for leaving, master. What reward will you give me for coming back?"

His eyes narrowed and he clenched his jaw. He held up the orbed toy.

"This, then this." He placed the toy on my lower back like he had with the U toy before I left and grasped his cock next, began to stroke it. Clear pre-cum dripped from the tip and slipped down the flared head. I licked my lips, wanting to taste it. I hadn't had an opportunity—yet—to do so, but we'd have the rest of our lives.

Picking up the vial of oil, he placed the opening of it at my entrance and carefully inserted it. I felt the warm oil fill me slowly, deeper and deeper. When done, he tossed the empty container to the side and picked up the toy, coated it with oil on his hand before pressing it to my back entrance.

"Relax, *gara*. Good girl." He was gentle, yet persistent, yet so was my body fighting it. I wasn't used to having something stretch me there and I clenched down. He tried and tried, but it was too much.

I was breathing hard and I had my face buried in the blankets. Tark stopped trying to work the toy into me and let it rest against me. And then, he turned it on.

"How about now?"

Of course the darn thing vibrated. *Everything* on Trion vibrated… and I liked it all.

I gasped at the feel of it, the echoes of the object moved through my body, sparking nerve endings to life. It mixed with the painful heat that radiated from my spanked bottom. I relaxed and Tark slid the toy in until the first orb shape disappeared inside me. The sensation was foreign, and exciting, and so naughty that of course my pussy grew even wetter. Panting now, I arched my back and looked over my shoulder at Tark. I wanted him, inside me, too. Right now.

He pushed my thighs wide, spreading me open. "You're so wet, *gara*. My cock is aching to get inside you."

I cried out at the feel of his fingers in my pussy and the vibrating top of the toy in my ass. As he continued to stroke me, he worked the toy in further and further until it was fully seated. Tark gave it a little tug to ensure it was seated well before he flipped me onto my back.

"Tark!" I cried as the base of it nudged into me.

"I believe the word I should be hearing from those pouty lips is master."

Using his knees to nudge my own wider, he settled into the cradle of my hips, his cock nudging at my entrance.

"Did you touch yourself when you were gone?" He pushed forward, spreading me wide, stretching me open.

My eyes fell closed and I groaned.

"Did you?" he repeated, his voice rough like ground rocks.

"Yes!" I cried, because he pulled back and thrust deeply, finally filling me up the way I needed it.

He tsked me. "I thought your pleasure belonged to me, *gara*."

"It does," I gasped. "I couldn't come. I couldn't come without you. I thought of you. Of this, of your cock in me and I tried, but nothing worked. Oh, God, it's so good."

I had never been so filled before. The combination of the toy and Tark's huge cock was enough to take me to the brink and over in only a few strokes. I'd been too needy for too long.

He crooned to me as I came, telling me how beautiful I was, how watching me come made him ready to come, too.

Once the fiery pleasure ebbed, he said, "I can't wait any longer. *Fark*, the vibration is too much. You're too much." He leaned in and kissed my neck, licked the sweaty skin there, rubbed his chest against my sensitive nipples.

His hips moved faster and more frantic. I was going to come again the way he hit my clit with every deep stroke. "Tark, master... please!"

"One more, Eva. We'll come together."

As he gripped my ass, I felt the pain of his palms against my sore flesh. He angled me up and thrust in hard, rubbing a spot inside me that made me come. Tark groaned as I milked and squeezed his cock. His shout was loud in my ear, but I didn't care. He was heavy on top of me, but I reveled in the heavy weight. It made me feel safe, and protected, and totally loved.

He lifted his hand and the vibrations in my ass and on my nipples ceased. I would have to learn how he did that. It was as if by magic. It felt like magic, this connection between us.

When Tark recovered enough to pull out, his seed slipped from me. He ran a finger through his sticky essence as he pulled the toy from me. I hissed out a breath at the feel of it, but missed it when it was gone.

"You are mine, *gara*."

He lowered his head, kissed me. Savored me. Tasted me.

Lifting his head, he met my gaze. I stroked the lock of hair back from his forehead and watched as it fell back in place.

"And you are mine. Tark. High councilor. *Master*."

THE END

BONUS: CHAPTER ONE OF *MATED TO THE WARRIORS*

Hannah Johnson, Interstellar Bride Processing Center, Earth

I was blindfolded, but I could hear the soft hum of several deep male voices whispering around me. I was surrounded. I turned my head left, then right, but I could see nothing, only blackness. Something silky smooth, but liquid like melted chocolate, enclosed my neck like a collar of liquefied heat. Once the circle was complete, my senses were enhanced. The scent of my mate's cock teased the air and I knew he stood before me. I could smell the spicy scent of his arousal. I knew well the exotic taste of his pleasure on my lips. How did I know his taste? How did I know the collar about my neck linked me to him somehow?

I tugged at my bonds, trying to reach him, to taste him, but the thick straps that held my wrists together above my head prevented me from doing so. The desire for my mates and the power of their link to me were strong, but all I could do was stand, naked, and wait.

The scent of my own skin and something strangely metallic flavored the air. I could feel the soft flow of slightly cool air moving over my naked flesh. My legs were in a wide stance. Pulling on the restraints above my head, I tried to step forward, but realized that thick straps around my ankles restrained my movement. I kicked at them, but found that although I had a few inches of leeway, beyond that, I could not budge.

All I could do was wait. My ears strained to hear footsteps, a rustle of clothing, anything to alert me to what was going to happen next. I was confused and uneasy, but my body was eager and aching for my mate's touch.

The thought sent me into a near panic, and my heart pounded so hard I was afraid it was going to explode out of my ribcage.

What was this? Why was I naked? Where the hell was I? This was not what I'd signed up for when I volunteered for the Interstellar Bride Program. I was supposed to be matched to a mate who would be perfect for me, and me alone. I was supposed to be cherished and loved, and...

As if I'd summoned him, a large hand settled on my shoulder and slid up to the side of my neck. Even blindfolded, I could feel the brute strength in that touch, and the sheer size of his palm made me tremble, but not with fear. I knew his touch, somehow, and craved more.

His voice filled my ear from behind, and he pressed the heat of his naked chest to my bare back.

"Do you accept my claim, mate? Do you give yourself to me and my second freely, or do you wish to choose another primary mate?" A deep, baritone voice growled the questions and my pussy grew wet in response to his voice. My mind didn't recognize him, but my body did.

"I accept your claim, warriors." The words flew past my lips, as if I had no control. And, in fact, I did not. I tried to ask a question, to find out where I was, what was going on, but it was like I was in a virtual reality sim. I could feel the heat of the giant male at my back. I could smell my mate's pre-cum teasing me with future pleasures. I could feel the unforgiving metal of the floor beneath my bare feet and the heated glide of liquid silk as it wrapped around my neck. I could hunger and ache and want, but I could not move.

Whatever was going to happen next was completely out of my control.

"Then we claim you in the rite of naming. You are mine and I shall kill any other warrior who dares to touch you." His hand squeezed softly, wrapping around my neck in the front, a soft but gentle reminder that he was the dominant one, that he could take me, fuck me, make me come—and there was nothing I could do about it.

I didn't want to escape that strength. I wanted more.

I'd chosen this, the Interstellar Bride Program and their selection testing. I vowed I would give my destined mate my trust and my life, utterly and without reservation.

He pressed his lips to the side of my face as the voices I'd heard chanting earlier answered him in a ritual sounding chorus of male voices. "May the gods witness and protect you."

My mate growled behind me and squeezed my throat the slightest bit with his right hand, and my pussy fluttered in welcome. A second pair of large male hands came to rest on the outsides of my thighs, and I knew then that another male knelt before me.

The hungry primary mate at my back held me tightly against his chest as my second man's rough tongue traced its way from the inside of my knee, up my inner thigh, to lick the wet core of me.

My hips jerked forward as his mouth clamped down on my clit. Two very large fingers slid into my pussy as he worked me into a frenzy with his mouth and tongue. I panted for breath and the growling behind me made my knees weak.

"You like his mouth on you?"

I knew, somehow, that he expected an answer, and that there would be no lying. "Yes."

"Come for us, then we will fuck you." His large cock nestled against my bare bottom and I was torn between the desire to press forward onto the sucking tongue that made me squirm, or push back hard to tease the cock pressed to my ass.

I tried to do both, but couldn't move. My captor kept one hand on my neck and another teasing one nipple, then the other, into tight peaks. He tugged them to the edge of pain as the man between my legs fucked me with his fingers and licked my clit so fast, he was better than any vibrator I'd ever used back home.

I moaned. I needed to be filled. Fucked. Claimed. Forever.

I exploded and pressed the back of my head into the giant chest behind me. He belonged to me now, my safe harbor, my mate. When my legs collapsed, he held me up, as I knew he would. He was mine, and I was his.

His voice was practically a purr in my ear. "Very good, we will fuck you now, mate. You belong to us."

Us. Yes. I wanted both of them. "Yes."

The man kneeling on the floor was mine, too. They were both mine.

My ankles were released and I was spun in a circle to face the male behind me. He lifted me off the floor and stepped back. I couldn't see as they freed my wrists. I lowered my arms, settled my wrists at my waist, grateful for the relief in my shoulders as my mate pulled me onto his lap facing him. I felt the huge head of his cock brush my core, and that was the only warning I received before he lifted me, then invaded me with one brutal stroke.

I cried out at the thick feel of him impaling me. He was huge!

I was stuffed so full my pussy ached and so aroused I couldn't think, I could only want. But before long, the familiar pleasurable heat of his pre-cum spread from my pussy to the rest of me and I squirmed, so hot and out of control that if he didn't move soon I was going to beg.

"Now, you shall be claimed. Forever."

His voice vibrated through my body and somehow, I knew what was coming as he leaned backward. He lay flat, pulling me down on top of him with my ass in the air.

Two hands landed on my bare bottom and held me with a firm, hungry grip. As I leaned forward over my mate, a second man squeezed heated oil into my virgin hole, and I whimpered.

This was what I'd been waiting for, what I'd wanted. What they'd been training me for.

My primary mate shifted below me, rubbing my clit over his hard body and I shuddered, so close to the edge that I felt like a wild animal, my entire focus on the joining of our bodies, and the thick glide of the second cock over my ass.

From behind me, a second voice, deep, solid, and reverent spoke to me. "Do you accept me, mate?"

"Yes!" I tried to lift my ass, to encourage him to move faster. His pre-cum traced a line of wetness on my bare ass cheek, then I felt the arousing fluid practically melt into my skin, driving me higher.

I lay flat on my mate's chest, my hands lifted to his face and waited for my other mate to breach me, to fill me, to make me truly complete.

My mate grabbed my knees and shifted under my legs, spreading my knees farther and bringing my ass up in perfect position for fucking. My knees were still bent, and as he supported my weight, I was bent over and ready for the second cock to fill me up.

"Hurry. Do it now."

Was that my husky voice? I didn't recognize the breathless sound, so filled with desperate hunger.

"I am pleased by your eagerness, but do not attempt to issue orders." A hand landed on my bare ass with a loud smack and I jerked in place as stinging heat spread straight from my ass to my clit. I wiggled my ass, wanting the man behind me to strike again. And again.

I licked my lips as my body clenched down on the cock filling my pussy. "Take me."

Smack.

"Fuck me," I begged.

Smack.

"*Please!*" I moaned as I thrust my hips back for the next strike of his palm. The mixture of pain and sizzling pleasure was incredible.

Smack.

"Please? Is that all you have to say to us?" My first mate asked the question with his cock buried balls deep inside me.

Oh, I knew what he wanted, and I was tempted to push him further, to feel the hot sting of their domination on my ass again and again. The flash of pain sparked my nerve endings and made my whole body tremble with lust. But I had pushed as far as I dared, and I was so aroused that my pussy actually throbbed, the need to come driving me to the brink of pain. I needed him—them—pounding into me. I needed to be completely filled. "Please, sir."

He didn't answer me with words, but some sign must have passed between them, for the thick head of my second mate's cock pressed against my tight little rosebud, penetrating the outer walls of my virgin ass with remarkable ease. I knew now that the training I'd been put through had been well worth it. The sound that left my throat was one I didn't recognize. After several careful yet masterful strokes, the man behind me stilled, his cock fully embedded in my ass.

I shattered into a million pieces at the connection, came apart and gave them everything. I didn't keep anything for myself.

I surrendered, completely. Wholly. My body belonged to them, my pleasure, my every breath.

As my body clenched and spasmed around their huge cocks, the scents and sounds started to fade, like I was walking through fog, slipping away until they were—gone.

I was alone. Empty.

My pussy clenching and pulsing around nothing.

I tried to curl into a ball, but couldn't move.

I drifted back to reality slowly, requiring several minutes

to emerge from a strange daze, to discover that I was strapped to a medical examination table in Earth's processing unit for the Interstellar Bride Program. I blinked, returning to myself, and to the woman I'd spent too much time with the last few days.

Warden Egara stared down at me with dark eyes and a program tablet in her hand. My body trembled with continued need as aftershocks of the orgasm still fluttered through my pussy. The exam table was cold and the gown I wore was open in the back. The standard gray cloth was covered with small replicas of the Interstellar Bride Program's insignia in a repeating pattern of red. I felt like I was wearing wallpaper.

"Very good, Hannah. The matching process is complete." Warden Egara was a stern-faced young woman who took her job, matching human women to their alien mates, very seriously. She looked at the medical equipment on the wall above my head and nodded to an assistant in a plain gray uniform who entered the room and began to remove the wires, tubes, and sensors they had attached to my head and body for the match assessment.

"What was that, a dream?" I licked my lips, parched from crying out my release. I wanted to know. A dream? A fantasy? Some deep, dark need I had buried so long ago that I didn't even know it existed? I'd just dreamt of being spanked and fucked, and not just by one man, but two. I'd also come harder than I ever had in my life.

"Oh, no, dear," the warden commented. "That was the recorded mating ritual of another human bride. That recording is several years old and belonged to a bride I sent there in the early days of the program." Warden Egara's face held a hint of a smile, the first I'd seen from her since entering the building for processing several days ago. She was very dedicated to her job. Very thoughtful, as if she had a personal interest in the happiness of every unmated warrior in the galaxy.

"You mean... I? That was... what?" What was I trying

to say? "That was real?"

"Oh, yes. The Neuroprocessing Units used by the matching system will be embedded in your body during final processing for transport. Not only does the NPU help you understand and speak their language, it has been preprogrammed to record your own mating ceremony so it can be properly documented and used to assist other brides in their own matching. Just like the other woman's experience was used to help match you."

I shuddered and wished she'd left me there, in that dreamland, for a few more minutes. I wanted more. Craved it. "Will my mate be like that?" Like what, I wasn't sure. I never got to see a face, but I knew. I *knew* I wanted him. Or them.

But two men? That was why I was confused.

"There were two men. Was I matched to two men?"

She shook her head. "No. You are only matched to one male. And your primary mate will be a warrior, but it will not be *that* warrior."

What did *primary mate* mean?

I shuddered and tried to imagine what might happen to me in the future. Would my mate be as big? As strong? Would I feel what that other bride felt? Would my mate want to include a second man in our mating ceremony? Would I want him to? What I had just experienced had gone beyond eagerness to total trust. Raw, mindless lust. Would I be as happy to be claimed as she had been?

I had never imagined being spanked before. I'd only thought of it as punishment, so I never would have volunteered for *that*. Truth be told, I didn't want to be matched to an alien mate at all. But, here I was, strapped to this freaking table in the processing center and it was my own fault. I'd volunteered for the Interstellar Bride Program to help get my brother out of debt with some very nasty people. He had three kids and a wife and if he didn't come up with a large sum of cash, they were all going to be on the streets. Or worse. Much worse.

My job as a preschool teacher barely paid me enough to survive on my own. I didn't have any extra money to give my brother. But I could do this.

Until this moment, I hadn't really believed there would be anything enjoyable in the matching process for me. I had doubted the bride program's ability to find a suitable match. I mean, really? How could a stupid computer program know which man in the entire galaxy would be perfect for me? I'd never found the right guy on Earth, so how could they find an alien match for me on a distant planet? The quivering pleasure I'd just experienced made me hopeful. *Very* hopeful. It was the first time in the past few weeks that I'd felt *maybe* things would be all right. Maybe volunteering for the Interstellar Bride Program hadn't been the biggest mistake of my life.

Mistake or not, family was family. This was the only way I could help my brother. My body and my life were all I had left of value. I wasn't rich, but I was young and fertile and unattached. Hell, uninspired was more like it. I'd had three lovers in five years, and none of them had made me come as hard as I just had… from a neural simulation. From another woman's memories.

Oh, God. I wanted one of those big, deep voices behind me. I wanted a huge hand wrapped and resting on my throat with a hot tongue stroking my clit. I wanted to be held in place as someone fucked me from behind. *I wanted…*

My monitor beeped and I blushed, knowing it was reading the increase in my heart rate as I relived everything that had just happened to me. No, it hadn't happened to me, but to her. The other woman. The one Warden Egara had sent to Prillon. The one who had been claimed by a warrior. A big, strong warrior with a huge cock. Her *primary mate*. Whatever that meant.

"So, is that where I've been matched? To that woman's planet?"

Warden Egara nodded curtly. "Yes. To a warrior of Prillon Prime."

Prillon Prime? I'd been matched to Prillon Prime? The planet inhabited by the hulking warrior race? The program's brochures had said that Prillon warriors actually requested brides while still in active military service. They were one of only three races that kept their brides with them on battleships. In space. On the front lines of the war between the biological races and the Hive, the artificial lifeforms and cyborg races trying to take over the universe. That war had finally come to Earth, and the coalition had accepted Earth under their protection, on one very strict condition.

Brides. A thousand a year. Most of Earth's brides came from the criminal justice system. Earth's politicians were not opposed to sacrificing *criminals* to fill the alien bride quota, but here I was, a volunteer hoping I hadn't just made the biggest mistake of my life.

I remembered reading that the Prillon males were supremely confident in their warriors' abilities to care for their mates. Anywhere. Prillon warriors never shied away from battle and were the most feared race in the Interstellar Coalition. They were on the front lines of the war, and their commanders were in charge of the entire interstellar fleet.

Holy shit. I wasn't going to a planet! I was going to go live on a spaceship in the middle of nowhere where they actually fought other spaceships? Or cyborgs. Or whatever! The heart rate monitor began beeping once again and this time it wasn't arousal I was feeling. It was panic.

I shook my head. Once, twice. "No. There must be some mistake."

"No mistake." She scowled at me. "Your match is estimated at ninety-nine percent compatibility."

"But…" I wanted to go to Forsia, or to the twin worlds of Ania and Axion, where they lived in cities surrounded by restaurants, parties, and opulence. I didn't want to go to a warship in *space*.

"Quiet." The word was bitten off as she hissed at me like an irritated cat. "It is done, the match complete. You already signed. Your family has been compensated, as you requested. Unless you wish to return the funds, you will honor your legal obligation to the program. You chose the matching protocol. You must abide by the results."

Warden Egara was nice enough, in her twenties and even pretty, if a bit brusque. I understood. The woman at the front desk told me that they didn't get many volunteers. Most of the women Warden Egara processed were convicted criminals whose only two choices were either enter the Interstellar Bride Program or serve hard time in prison.

"Hmm. I believe I will add this outburst to your bride data. Your new mate should be warned of your impertinence."

My eyes widened and my mouth fell open.

"Just a minute! I never agreed to that." Impatient, I yanked at a couple of sticky pads attached to my temples and grimaced as they snagged on my long black hair. I handed them to the assistant, who finished unhooking me from the rest of it and left the room. Warden Egara must have realized that I was about to shove that tablet up her ass, for she held out her hand in a placating gesture.

"All right, Miss Johnson. I will delete that from your profile." She tapped the screen again and frowned. Her long hair was pulled into a tight bun and the strain on her skin made her look even more severe. "Now, for the record, state your name."

I took a deep breath, let it out. "Hannah Johnson."

"Miss Johnson, are you now, or have you ever been married?"

"No."

"Do you have any biological offspring?"

"No." I rolled my eyes. They'd already asked me this. I'd signed this shit in triplicate and I was sure it was listed on her tablet.

"Excellent." She tapped her screen a few times without looking at me. "I am required to inform you, Miss Johnson, that you will have thirty days to accept or reject the mate chosen for you by our matching protocols." She lifted her head and actually grinned at me. "Judging by these scores, however, I think that is highly unlikely."

I wasn't as confident in the computer program they used to match brides to their mates, but I was reassured that the ultimate decision was mine. "Okay."

"Regardless of your choice, there will be no return to Earth. If your new mate is unacceptable, you may request a new primary mate after thirty days… on Prillon Prime. You may continue this process until you find a mate who is acceptable."

"Warden, I just want to know…"

She sighed. "You have already signed the documents, Miss Johnson, but I also feel obligated to remind you that as of this moment, you are no longer a citizen of Earth, but a warrior bride of Prillon Prime, and, as such, you shall be bound by the laws and customs of your new world."

"But—"

"You have been matched, Hannah, to one of the fiercest warriors from that world. You should be proud. Serve him well." I wasn't sure if Warden Egara's command was meant to encourage me or frighten me, but I didn't have long to wonder. I had no idea that she knew anything personal about the alien males she matched. Apparently, she knew more than I did. Perhaps she liked me more than I imagined. If I were a crazy serial killer, would she still send me to this fierce warrior? Did she tell all women some lie about how fantastic their match was to make them eager to leave Earth?

She stepped forward and shoved on the side of my medical chair. With a small jolt, a bright blue opening appeared in the side of the wall. Still strapped securely, I could do nothing as a long, very large needle appeared. The needle was attached to a long metallic arm in the wall. I tried to pull back and she raised her voice so I could hear her over the bubbling of the strange blue liquid below me.

"Do not fight it, Hannah. That device will simply implant your permanent NPUs. Nothing to fear." Her smile was forced and her lips thin, but at least she was trying to reassure me. I got the feeling she didn't do this kind of warm and fuzzy thing often.

I slid into the tiny enclosure and felt the sting of the needle first on one side of my temple, then the other. I was quite sure that the strange and very strong buzzing sensation I now felt on both sides of my head would give me a migraine from hell. Resigned to suffer the effects of the NPU, I was lowered into a heated bath of some sort. Blue light surrounded me.

"When you wake, Hannah Johnson, your body will have been prepared for Prillon Prime's matching customs and your mate's requirements. He will be waiting for you."

Holy shit. "Now? Right now?" I struggled against the cuffs that held my wrists to the table. "I haven't even said goodbye to my brother! Wait!"

For some reason, my anger and frustration just disappeared, as if the warm bath washed it away. What the heck was in the water? I felt so relaxed, so happy.

So numb.

Warden Egara's clipped voice was the last thing I heard above the quiet humming of electrical equipment and lights. "Your processing will begin in three... two... one..."

Everything faded to black.

STORMY NIGHT PUBLICATIONS WOULD LIKE TO THANK YOU FOR YOUR INTEREST IN OUR BOOKS.

If you liked this book (or even if you didn't), we would really appreciate you leaving a review on the site where you purchased it. Reviews provide useful feedback for us and for our authors, and this feedback (both positive comments and constructive criticism) allows us to work even harder to make sure we provide the content our customers want to read.

If you would like to check out more books from Stormy Night Publications, if you want to learn more about our company, or if you would like to join our mailing list, please visit our website at:

www.stormynightpublications.com

Made in the USA
Coppell, TX
20 February 2023

13120378R00089